To Stephanie

Happy
reading!

DEVIANT
FLUX

A DURGA SYSTEM NOVELLA
JESSIE KWAK

Jessie Kwak

DEVIANT FLUX

A DURGA SYSTEM NOVELLA

JESSIE KWAK

For my cousins,
I love you all.

1

STARLA

The air here is thick with memories.

Starla Dusai breathes deep the sharp tang of oil and sweat, the sweet musk of antifreeze and unwashed bodies passed through the recycler too many times to count: Maribi Station smells like home.

At least, it's the closest she's found since she watched Alliance missiles shatter her family home into stars five years ago.

There are differences, of course. For one, there are too many people here, bodies crowded into every corner, in every corridor and doorway, brushing past her from every direction. The air is more electric than in her childhood home of Silk Station, too, geared towards entertaining the thousands of travelers who arrive here to catch shuttles deeper out into the black or farther into Durga's Belt, or who are waiting for the bigger transports to shuttle them back to the surface of one of the two sunward planets, Indira or New Sarjun.

On Silk Station there was breathing room — even when her parents' ship was in port and Silk Station swelled with crew, it was all family. And in her new planetside home on New Sarjun, Starla can go for hours without seeing another soul if she wants. In a way, her godfather's home ebbs and flows just as Silk Station did, especially in the past few years with his soldiers and hired mercenaries flooding in and out, thudding footsteps and the tang of blood in the dry air waking Starla more than once in the middle of the night.

She's taking the long way to meet Gia at the boxing gym, through Terminal A, which is doubly packed with people this close to the shift change. Starla hopes this will give her better odds of finding the one person she's desperate to find — even if the press of people is making it more difficult to actually pick an individual out of the crowd.

She hadn't counted on the newcomers. Terminal A isn't just packed with station inhabitants today. A ferry from elsewhere in Durga's Belt has just docked, judging by the glut of travelers shouldering duffel bags and stopping in the middle of the passage to frown at the station transit maps and mouth questions to each other.

Starla slips through them, ignoring the few that seem to ask her for directions.

Her comm buzzes with a message from Gia.

YOU SKIPPING TRAINING?

Starla's beginning to regret coming this way. She thought heading through a large swath of the population would give her a better chance of spotting her target, but it's just chaos, a constant swarm of people.

It's hard to take it all in.

The terminal's length is lined with shopping and entertainment, callers beckoning from the neon-clad doorways of casinos and brothels and bars — a heady pulse thrums through Starla's chest as she passes one, and she catches a glimpse of a room packed with bodies and smoke and flashing lights, the mass of people dancing. For Starla, it's just after lunch. But in such a transient place, you can choose your own time.

So long as you keep moving, it seems. In the stream of Terminal A, she can't find a single spot to just stand for one second and type out a reply to Gia without being in the way. Somebody always needs to get by, or set something where you're standing, or open the door you didn't notice behind you.

It makes her skin crawl. Silk Station didn't use to make her skin crawl — it fit like a glove. Is it this station in particular? Or is it that she's become used to wide open spaces after five years living on New Sarjun?

Gia's message blinks insistently at the edge of her field of vision.

She sidesteps a hawker in religious headgear who clutches at her arm and tries to hand her a saint token, saying something to her around blue-painted teeth. Starla brushes the woman back and slips into the lee of a pile of crates for a second's breather, grabs her comm.

BE THERE IN 5.

She pushes Send; Gia's message disappears from her heads-up.

Gia has a thing about timeliness that Starla should probably try to emulate, but she can't be bothered this trip. Despite being comfortable with the station's layout, she keeps misjudging the time it will take her to get through Maribi's labyrinth — and she's always hesitant to leave off her search.

Because her cousin Mona is here, she knows it. And in her imagination, every instant she turns away from an open doorway, Mona walks past. Near misses, it has to be — she's been all over this damned station.

And she's running out of time.

BE HERE IN 2. HAD ANY LUCK?

Gia's response blinks on the bottom of Starla's heads-up. Starla swipes it away without responding, because, no, she hasn't had any luck. Anyway, Starla can tell Gia in person when she gets to the boxing gym. In five.

Starla stops to scan the terminal, turns to find a woman in a forklift suit yelling at her. Probably to get out of the way so she can get to the crates; words blink at the bottom of her heads-up, the unit's attempt to transcribe the forklift operator's diatribe. It's coming out garbled — maybe she's got an accent, maybe it's too loud for the unit to work properly.

Or maybe she's using too many expletives. One thing Starla has realized on this trip with Gia is that the software isn't programmed to transcribe swear words. She'll have to fix that.

Starla waves both hands at the forklift operator — *All right, all right.* — and ducks back into the throng. She keeps scanning the people passing, out of habit, but doesn't see anyone who looks like her cousin.

After five years of searching, she's seen nothing of her

family but obituaries. Auntie Faye's ship was shot down shortly after the attack on Silk Station. Amit was picked up by the Alliance and has since disappeared. Uncle Ro was cornered on the volcanic moon Pele, shot himself before he could be arrested. Deyva hasn't been heard from in years and is presumed dead.

Her parents and countless others died in the initial attack.

So when one of her godfather's smuggling contacts saw someone matching the description of Starla's cousin, Mona, working on Maribi Station, Starla had to see for herself — and fast.

There are still a few bounties on the boards for missing members of the Silk Station diaspora, and others are out there hunting her cousins, her aunts, her uncles. It's what worries Starla the most, that maybe the reason she hasn't found any of them is because they're being snatched up by bounty hunters first, trundled into cargo holds and whisked off into secret Alliance prisons.

Like she'd been shipped off to Redrock Prison right after the attack. She'd had the help of her godfather, Willem Jaantzen, to escape, and now she'll do anything she can to help the others.

If she can find them.

But there are dozens more Alliance prisons throughout the Durga System.

And a hundred more hub stations like Maribi bored into Durga's Belt and Bixia Yuanjin's moons.

It doesn't matter. Starla will find Mona, even if she has to open every door in this place.

A change in the current of foot traffic catches her attention. Somewhere up ahead, the crush of people is getting more packed on the edges, and individuals are looking up and turning back around, slipping into open doorways, making themselves scarce.

Starla's been paying so much attention to the faces of the people around her that she's nearly in the middle of it before she realizes what's going on: an Indiran Alliance squadron marching through the center of Terminal A, five soldiers with hands on weapons like they think Maribi is theirs to police — or like they're expecting to stir up trouble. Their riot visors are down and scanning the crowd, and Starla's mouth goes dry.

She knows what they're scanning for. Known criminals. Terrorist group members. Exiled freedom fighters. The daughters of notorious pirate families.

She tries not to look frantic, tries to blend in, but she's caught at the edge of the crowd — even those who aren't on an Alliance wanted list aren't too keen to mix up with a troop like this. If she runs, if she pushes through, she'll only attract more attention.

But in a second she'll be face to face with the soldiers, and that close, their facial recognition will uncover her for sure.

She'd rather run and look suspicious than get caught — but as she tenses, someone grabs her from behind, pulls her through an open doorway and out of sight.

A hand clamps over her mouth, though Starla doesn't think she's cried out. Gia's been training her well, though, and Starla breaks free in seconds, spins to meet her attacker.

She doesn't recognize the woman's face at first, not with

the wild mane of magenta hair and the scar slashed across her nose and cheek. But she would recognize the way those hands formed her namesign anywhere.

"Starla," she signs, "it's okay. It's me."

Mona.

2

GIA

Giaconda Áte is not a fan of space.

She admittedly doesn't get out much back home, but after two weeks either in a transport or on Maribi Station, she's realizing how nice it is to know that she can. To know that she could go hiking in the desert plateaus around Bulari, or even hop on a train and head out into the hinterlands around the capital, visit some podunk town or other whose name she's only seen stamped on shipping crates and freight trains. Get wild and drive out to the family farm, see if anyone from the old commune is still alive and kicking around.

Here, it's like living in a coal mine, all tunnels and cables and tight spaces and too many sallow people. She's never realized how necessary it is to have a horizon — combine that with the knowledge that if you walk too far up, down, left, or right, you're through an airlock and drifting.

Gia feels the loss of possible directions like a missing limb.

She checks the address on the doorway to the Manilan

coffee place, notes with disappointment that she's still a few numbers shy. She'll have to come back later, because she could use the caffeine boost and this place smells amazing — coffee, cardamom, orange, honey. It looks like the sort of place that would help her unwind.

She can't even remember what being unwound feels like.

In a way, that's part of this trip. Head off-planet to keep Starla out of trouble, take in the underwhelming sights of Maribi Station, and forget for a minute about how she's spent the past few years digging bullets out of her friends and putting them into her enemies. After a mess like an all-out war, a girl needs a getaway. Needs to drink a cup of decent coffee without worrying that it's too quiet, too crowded, an ambush, a trap.

Back home on New Sarjun, it's a fresh new world. The losers of Bulari's underground civil war between the crime families have been killed or pushed into exile, and the rest of the families are licking their wounds and sniffing at new opportunities. The lingering atmosphere of grief and opportunism is almost as exhausting as the war had been, so when Jaantzen needed someone to go with Starla to find some long-lost cousin on Maribi Station, damn sure Gia had leapt at the chance.

The next stall in this row of restaurants is a respectable-looking empanada joint: sweet corn pastries stuffed with vat shrimp and curry. It also smells amazing. And the address is also a few numbers shy. Dammit.

She's on one of the lowest levels of Maribi Station, and despite the bustle of people and heat from the kitchens, Gia can't shake the chill. Mentally, she knows there's no difference between the heart of an asteroid and a spaceship, but it feels like being buried.

Maribi Station wasn't founded by a corporation like most of the larger outposts in Durga's Belt. Instead, it began as a scrappy claim settlement, with prefab units glued to the asteroid's surface while miners tunneled below, eventually fortifying the tunnels they dug and boosting the number of services and amenities on offer until it became the unmatched transit and shipping hub it is today.

Because of this, it's not a slick company town like so many of the others are, impossible to break into for business unless you have an ID number with the Alliance. Instead, control of Maribi has fallen into the hands of one main family, which acts as an umbrella organization for a whole host of smaller operations on the station. Want to start a competing operation? You'll find yourself out an airlock in no time. But if you have an idea for a complementary business, you're welcome pay tribute to the Maribi Cartel.

Problem is, when a group like the Maribi Cartel has no competition — either for control of the station, or from other nearby shipping hubs — they start to think they can do things like double tariffs and docking fees. Maybe that worked while the families of New Sarjun were occupied trying to murder each other, but now things are back to normal, and something's got to be done.

That's the second reason Gia is here: to be Jaantzen's representative at tomorrow's meeting of interested stakeholders from the planets of New Sarjun and Indira, and a smattering of other outposts in Durga's Belt. Some of the biggest names in organized crime throughout the system are here to do a little collective bargaining.

But first, she's got a one-on-one with a local shipping operator who's not with the cartel. It doesn't hurt to gather other allies, in case the cartel isn't interested in negotiations.

She finally matches the address to a deli two doors down from the empanada restaurant. Its plastic backlit menu is cracked in half, the lower half unlit, and reads like a mugshot lineup of humanity's most uninspired sandwiches. Skimming through the options, Gia can almost taste the wilted lettuce and flavorless soy shawarma.

"What do you want?" growls a young tough leaning in the doorway. Literally nothing about the deli is a customer magnet, but this guy and his buddy, who's playing solitaire at the bistro table just outside the door, ensure that no one could possibly mistake it for a dining option.

"I'm here to see Lorn," she says, and that sparks a round of cagey glances from the toughs.

"That right." The solitaire kid slaps another card onto the bistro table.

Gia crosses her arms, gives them both a look that says she doesn't have time for shit and neither does Lorn, whoever he represents.

"I can come back later," Gia says. "Got all the time in the world, only it seems like Lorn thought it was urgent. I guess you can explain this to him, though."

That gets another look, and finally the tough in the doorway pushes off his lean, lazy like he's been planning to get up at this particular moment anyway. He's half her age and lanky as a string bean — they all are out here — but it's clear he's been training those low-G muscles.

Gia's not here to fight — and looking for a fight in every gesture is another relic of the past few years of civil war she needs to let go of.

Chill, girl. Be chill.

The lanky youth pushes open the door and pauses halfway in, mumbles something to someone on the other side. Glances back at Gia as though evaluating her. Says something else through the doorway.

Finally he turns, pushing the door all the way open with a whipcord arm. "You can go in," he says.

"Thank you kindly." Gia gives him a tight smile, then steps past; he hasn't left her much room and she wrinkles her nose at the reek of his cologne. If she catches a whiff of that on her shirt later, she's gonna be pissed. He grins down at her. She rolls her eyes.

The restaurant is empty. When Gia walks in, the cook behind the window gives her a quick look, then suddenly remembers he needs to be elsewhere. Something's sizzling, smells like burning onions and rancid fryer oil; Gia feels the cloud of it sinking into her pores. Forget the cologne. She's gonna smell like *this* place for the rest of the day.

The inside of the deli is claustrophobic, just like everything on this station. She'd suspected she was in the outskirts of this level, and since the far wall of the kitchen is literally dug-out rock, her suspicions are confirmed.

The thought makes her shudder.

There's a lunch counter outside the kitchen window, a row of booths across from the lunch counter. Only one of them's doing business: a single man, a pair of chipped coffee mugs, and a carafe.

"We're all just on a ball of rock hurtling through space," the man says; he's seen her reaction to the dug-out asteroid wall in the kitchen. "Some of us are just forced to acknowledge it more than others. And as far as I understand, getting tossed out into your Jupari Desert will kill a person almost as fast as getting pushed out an airlock here."

"You're most comfortable with what you know, I guess," Gia says, shoulders relaxed, guard up. It's not the most pleasant conversation opener, but is it a threat? Or just what passes for small talk on Maribi?

The man waves a hand for her to join him.

"Coffee?" he asks, palming the carafe as if to pour.

A rainbow of oils swirl on the surface of the brown liquid in his cup.

"I'm off the stuff," Gia says. The stuff he's got in his cup, at least. "You Lorn?"

"That's right."

Gia slips into the booth across from him and takes a good look.

Lorn is an olive-skinned middle-aged man with a paunch and a receding hairline, looking more like a bookkeeper than the surly soldier she was expecting. He's got that sallow cast to his face that says he lives in space and can't afford a VitD bed, the pinched look she's beginning to suspect comes from the constantly seeping chill you feel on Maribi Station, no matter what the temperature actually is.

Doesn't help that the booth is little more than a metal bench, the paint peeling off. Not designed to sit in for long;

Gia's been here thirty seconds and the bones in her ass are already complaining. Good thing this guy Lorn has some extra padding there to help him out.

"I appreciate your time," he says. "My apologies about the secrecy."

"I take it you don't work for the Maribi Cartel."

A tight smile, so fast she's not sure she saw it. "No, Ms. Áte. I don't work for anyone. But I belong to a group that can help Mr. Jaantzen achieve his goals."

She hates this kind of cryptic talk — she's not Manu, Jaantzen's silver-tongued lieutenant — but she forces herself to relax. "Tell me more," she says, figuring polite is always a good move at the beginning. You can always escalate from there if you're feeling feisty, but it's harder to get back to civility if you start off cranky.

"I understand you're here to negotiate a better shipping deal with the cartel for Mr. Jaantzen," Lorn says. "What tariff rate did your boss pay on his last shipment?"

Gia lifts an eyebrow. "No offense, but I'd like to know a bit more about you," she says.

"Thirty-seven percent," Lorn says. "Up from twenty-five percent on the one before. Did you know the cartel charges a different rate to everyone who ships goods through Maribi?"

This is news to Gia, and apparently Lorn can see it on her face because he nods, satisfied. "And that's not even just a number handed down from the cartel — it all depends on who in the docks wants to take their cut, figuring your boss is too far away to complain and doesn't have any other good options when it comes to shipping his goods. It's greed, of course. And prejudice."

If Lorn is expecting her to ask whether the cartel's lackeys are prejudiced against Jaantzen for being from New Sarjun, being lowborn, or just being a newer player to the game, he'll be disappointed. Gia just raises an eyebrow.

"If you don't believe me, just ask some of your fellow delegates, if you have any you trust. The Yangs paid thirty-two percent last time, the Demosgas only eighteen."

"Prices get negotiated differently," says Gia, though the discrepancy is sharp — and it's no wonder Julieta Yang is so fiery pissed about this whole thing if she's paying nearly double what Aiax Demosga is. "And I'm here to take it up with them directly."

"Not to mention the docking fees," Lorn says, like he didn't hear her. "Or, rather, the bribes certain crew bosses in the docks skim off the top for themselves." He drinks his coffee; the nerve-grating slurp is a negotiation tactic all its own.

"What do you have to say to me?" Gia asks.

Lorn just sets his mug back down. "I expected Mr. Jaantzen to come to Maribi himself."

"He doesn't like to leave the planet," Gia says. And even if he did, with all the reconciliation and restructuring necessary in the wake of the civil war, he's got his hands full.

"Or maybe his lieutenant, Mr. Juric."

Gia tenses at that, not sure if he's probing for information or simply making conversation. "He's busy," she says. Though in truth she's not yet sure if Manu will ever walk again. The last few months of the war did their damage.

Lorn takes another sip of coffee; the rainbow oil slick swirls.

"We've been hearing rumors of trouble back in Bulari."

"We've had some disagreements. Seems to be cleared up now."

"We've heard that Willem Jaantzen is a troublemaker."

"He's a trouble solver," Gia says. "Tell me why I'm here."

Lorn nods slowly, runs a pudgy finger around the rim of his coffee cup. "If we're going to be making deals," he says, "we want to be sure we're making them with the right person."

"Glad to hear it. Because if you want to keep chatting I can go find you a therapist. You want to make a deal, spit it out."

"Ten percent, no dock fees. Guaranteed for five years."

Gia raises an eyebrow. "Who are you to offer that? You're not with the cartel."

Lorn shakes his head, slow. "The cartel is yesterday's news," he says. "We're the next wave of power on Maribi. And we're offering Mr. Jaantzen the best deal he'll get on this rock. Or in Durga's Belt."

"In exchange for?"

"We need funds to finish what we've started. All we're asking is a year's estimated tariffs, prepaid."

Gia laughs. It would be a fantastic deal if there was any chance of it being true. The Maribi Cartel rule their station with an iron fist, and have done for as long as she's been alive. Its leaders have lived through riots and backstabbings and attempted coups and have come out stronger than ever, time after time. And this accountant-looking fellow is going to take them down?

He's furrowed his brow, offended, and she waves a hand: *No offense.*

"Man, I don't mean nothing by it. But we're not gonna just give you a hundred thousand credits and see if it works out. Even if you put your neck out by meeting with me."

Lorn tips back the rest of his oily coffee. Grounds cling to the rim; he grimaces and wipes his mouth with the back of his hand. "I'm a ghost, Ms. Áte; you won't find me again unless I want you to. Tell the cartel someone's plotting against them and they'll yawn — it happens all the time. You have until first shift tomorrow to talk with your boss and get his answer. If you gamble and we win, it's an eyewatering deal. If you keep your cards off the table and we win, you'll want to find another shipping hub."

Like there is another shipping hub this convenient.

"Jaantzen doesn't take kindly to extortion and threats."

"I'd much rather it be an investment offer."

"And that's all there is to the deal."

Lorn gives her a small, private smile. "Only that when the disruption goes down, you remember who your boss placed his bets with, Ms. Áte."

Oh.

He wants her to fight for him, whoever he is. There's not even a chill in Gia's gut at the thought, not after the routine horrors of the past two years. It's just a dull, aching sickness, like bad vodxx on a stomach gone too far past the point of hunger.

If he's done even a touch of research on Jaantzen he'll know she's one of his best fighters and his most skilled surgeon — an asset anyone would need on their side during a war.

An asset she very badly does not want to be.

Every fiber of her being screams to get on the first boat out of here — doesn't matter where it's going, so long as it's not another war zone, so long as she's not just another hired gun in just another never-ending fight. But she tamps that down as a trick of the oily stench of this place. She may have taken Sulila oaths to do no harm when she earned her doctor's badge, but Jaantzen doesn't pay her for her flawed conscience or cloudy, cracked morality. That path forked years back, and Gia took the wrong turn.

At least this time she's not going to be expected to watch everyone she loves be carved up and broken. At least this time it's just strangers.

"I'll talk to Jaantzen."

She holds out a hand to shake, then rises. She needs to get to the gym before Starla misses her, and out of the deli before the oil-impregnated air causes her face to break out like a teenager. This place seems smaller even than when she walked in — it clamps around her like a vise and she's half hoping one of the young toughs at the door gives her enough lip that she feels justified punching him in the face.

"We'll be in touch before first shift tomorrow," Lorn says.

He stays in the booth, opens his comm, pours himself another cup of rancid coffee as though settling in to do some work. Gia pushes through the door and into relatively fresh air as fast as she can, walking past the toughs like they're furniture.

Back out in the corridor, far from the deli, Gia checks her comm and doesn't see a message from Starla asking where she's at. Which means Starla is probably also late for their date at the gym.

You skipping training? she messages.

The screen blinks, message read.

Be there in 5.

That means fifteen, Gia knows from experience. Add to that a few minutes for Starla to get changed and warm up on her own, and Gia still has plenty of time to get her own ass to the gym.

Be here in 2. Had any luck?

The screen blinks as the message is read; Starla doesn't answer.

Panic spikes Gia's gut, but she takes a deep breath. They're not in Bulari, where for the last years danger has lurked around every corner. Starla's fine. Gia will head to the gym, only a few minutes late, and by the time she gets there the girl will be gearing up to practice.

She has to be.

3

STARLA

Mona's signing is rusty, like her fingers need a drop of oil in the joints or her brain needs some dust brushed out of years-old neural pathways so the words flash through rather than catch and snag on the barbs.

"I can't believe you found me," Mona signs.

And Starla gives her a *Wait, what?* look. "You just found me," she signs.

"I've been watching. Those Alliance assholes just got here," Mona signs, and if Starla has had any doubts that this woman is her cousin they're dashed aside by the nonsense sign Mona uses for the Indiran Alliance, the rude one she and Starla made up when they were kids.

Mona's hair still grows long and coarse, curls still tangled and frizzy even though they're now a magenta that practically glows in the neon hologram lights from the brothel behind them. Her girlish freckles are still there, only intensified, constellations scattered across her nose and cheeks. She's still thin, with that tall grace that comes from being raised off-planet, though it's entirely more common here than on New Sarjun. Starla doesn't realize how much she missed not standing out for her own height.

But Mona's changed, too. An old scar cuts across her chin, and another slashes at the same angle across her cheek and the bridge of her nose, the thin line of Durga's Belt slicing through a backdrop of stars. She wears makeup, done like she's well practiced, but Starla's seen makeup cover scars like that easily, and Mona isn't trying.

Starla's fortunate that the Alliance assumes she's dead; there's no bounty on her head to tempt one of Jaantzen's associates into giving up the location of a girl no one has really deemed a threat in the end. Not like there had been on some of her family members who've been captured and murdered in the past five years.

Even so, she looks different, just like Mona does. Keeps her hair cut close and spiky, and lately she's been taking to thick black eyeliner to see if Jaantzen says anything. He gives it a second look sometimes when he thinks she won't notice, but she's pushed enough buttons by this point to know he'll never bring it up.

Not like Raj Dusai would have.

But now's not the time to think about that.

"You and I need to stay out of sight," Mona signs. "I'm glad I found you in time."

"You knew I was here? Where have you been?"

"Watching. I heard someone was asking about me. Wanted to be sure." Mona jerks her chin at the door to the terminal beyond, where the Alliance squadron is still working the crowd. "Can't be too careful."

"The Alliance; I thought they didn't come here." It was one of the reasons Jaantzen had agreed to let her come, that Maribi Station was, well, not hostile to the Alliance. But unwelcoming. And he certainly wouldn't have sent Gia — shit. Starla dug out her comm, held up a finger to Mona.

RAN INTO TROUBLE, AM FINE. FOUND

Mona snatches the comm out of her hands before she can finish the message.

"Who?" Mona asks.

"A friend." Starla holds out her hand for the comm, but Mona slips it into her pocket.

"We need to talk first."

A thread of unease has been winding itself around Starla's gut, tickling faintly at first. Now it's cinching tighter, more insistent. This woman is her cousin, there's no doubt about that. But it's been almost six years. Who has her cousin become?

"The comm," Starla signs sharply. "Give it to me."

But Mona just crooks a finger at her and spins like a dancer, magenta curls whirling out from her shoulders as she darts back into the crowd.

Starla doesn't hesitate.

Whatever's going on, she didn't come all this way just for Mona to flash in and out of her vision like a mirage. And anyway, she's got a few more minutes at least before Gia completely freaks out.

She follows the bobbing magenta curls.

Mona doesn't slow, only gives a quick glance over her

shoulder to see if Starla's following her. She's weaving through the throng of people with subtle side steps and bobs like she's been navigating these crowds for years. Starla pushes, less gracefully, always just missing threading the eye of the needle behind her cousin.

Once, Mona checks her own comm, then reaches back to pull Starla into a souvenir shop. They stay there until the pair of Alliance troopers has passed.

"How did you — "

But Mona just winks and continues on.

Who is this woman? Starla knows people change, and she expected Mona to have shifted and grown like anyone else. Starla knows she's done her fair share of changing herself since coming to live with Jaantzen on New Sarjun.

But this woman is confident and unapologetic, decisive. Not the cousin Starla remembers always looking over her shoulder for authorities while Starla dragged them into trouble. The vivid hair looks amazing, warming her cool olive skin, but it's not a color the Mona of Starla's memories would have chosen. That Mona wore grays and blacks, painting herself in the invisible tones of her surroundings in an effort not to be noticed among the throngs of family members. As a result, she was always missing, even when she was in the room — people asking Starla where she'd gone while Starla frowned, puzzled, and pointed to where Mona was curled on a cushion in the corner with her book.

This Mona stands out in a crowd. And that scar . . .

Mona leads her down a staircase past the platform for Maribi's one rickety orbital tram, down three levels to where the rooms have been partially carved from the heart of the asteroid. This floor is part of an entertainment district, but at once seedier and more relaxed than the casinos and bars lining the terminal. Fewer flashing lights, no callers gesticulating in the doorway. Just guttering electric signs announcing Live Dancers, Cold Drinks, Hot Noodles, Cheap Rooms.

Starla's only been on this rock for a few days, but she's starting to know her way around — much better than Gia. Maribi Station is a mining resupply hub built into an asteroid, a transient place built in layers spreading out and down from the docks: entertainment, supply shops, medical bays. Gia's used to navigating cities spread flat, not ones that burrow and cling and climb, passageways winding in on themselves like tangles of cable.

Starla's sense of direction was honed on an asteroid station, though. The Alliance may have destroyed her home, but they can't take that from her.

Mona slips through a doorway edged by a projected holo-gram that gives Starla the stomach-clenching feeling that she's standing at the edge of an open airlock, staring into the glit-tering void, ready to let go. Beyond the doorway is only black, illuminated by a scattering of stars and the words *The Nebula* drifting, pulsing neon pink, across the entrance.

Starla pushes through the words; her feet appear to be stepping on nothing.

She takes another step, feeling a giddy rush in the pit of her stomach as the floor seems to drop into oblivion, a startled lurch of confusion when her foot connects with the floor. A few patrons near the door glance up with bored disinterest. They must watch a lot of newbies walk through that door.

Holographic space scenes are projected over gleaming

black lacquer walls and floors; for a moment, Starla feels like she's floating, remembers her one stolen space walk years ago, as a teenager when her family was still alive, drifting among the stars while Mona watched timid behind the airlock doors.

Mona's watching her from the bar, grinning.

Starla's soul soars, her heart thrumming with giddiness — and the rhythm of whatever music is playing.

It must be loud; patrons are shouting conversations to each other with gaping jaws while only two feet away. The bartender's bobbing her head just slightly in time to whatever music is playing, black braids wound in an intricate crown, silver-and-turquoise rings outlining both eyebrows.

Mona leans in to ask something — she's angled away from Starla, and Starla's heads-up doesn't bother trying to transcribe over the racket in the bar.

The bartender just shrugs and shakes her head, chin still bobbing to the music. Another question gets an affirmative, and the bartender hands them two weak, overcarbonated local brews, served in sipping bulbs as though they're really in zero G. Mona hands one to Starla and leads her to a low table in the corner of the room. It looks like a glowing asteroid, slowly spinning through the cosmos beneath their glasses.

"Here's a place we can talk," she signs as soon as she's set her drink down.

The effect of this place is so good, Starla almost expects the bulb to drift back up. But, no. They're still on Maribi. Gravity holds.

A thousand questions crowd Starla's mind. Where has Mona been this whole time? What happened to her face? Did anyone else survive?

But there's something she needs to take care of first. Gia needs to know about the Alliance.

"The comm," she signs. "I need it."

Mona nods, but doesn't pull it out of her pocket.

"Your friend, who is she?"

"She works for — " Starla's hands hesitate at *godfather*. "My boss." She fingerspells his name, Willem Jaantzen, and Mona just shrugs like she's never heard of him. Probably true, out here — back home, everybody knows who Jaantzen is.

"Do you trust her?"

"I do. I need to warn her about the Alliance."

"If she's smart she'll be fine."

Starla just holds out her hand for the comm.

"I need to know I can trust you."

Starla doesn't have a response to that. Her own cousin? The years they've spent together, the trouble they've gotten into. The years Starla has spent trying to find Mona, trying to pull her back into the fold. What has she gotten into?

Mona must see the look of shock on her face, because she pushes her palms out. "Calm down. I mean I just need to know." She leans back in her chair like she's relaxed, like the last five years hadn't happened.

Like she isn't holding Starla hostage.

Starla shrugs, stands. "I'll find you later," she signs.

She's halfway to the door when Mona catches her: fingernails light above her right elbow, Starla would recognize the touch anywhere.

Mona presses the comm into Starla's palm. "I'm sorry. I'm sorry. Sit. I trust you."

People are watching, surreptitious glances that prick Starla's skin with heat, but she doesn't sit, not yet.

I'M FINE, she types, hits send. Then: WATCH OUT FOR ALLIANCE, PATROLS HERE. I FOUND MONA. WE'RE SAFE.

The reply comes before she even gets back to her seat.

HOTEL. NOW.

SOON, WERE SAFE. AT THE NEBULA LEVEL 15 DONT COME. SEE YOU SOON.

Starla expects another sharp command in answer, but her comm stays dark. She slides it into her pocket, then leans back in her own seat and looks at her cousin, evaluating where they might go from here.

"Okay. Let's talk."

"This place, I love it," Mona signs, fingers making fluttering motions at the twinkling, floating stars. One drifts past her nose, glittering in her hazel eyes. "And it's safe. I just want to talk."

"Me too."

"What are you doing here?"

"Looking for you." What does Mona think she's doing? "Did you know I was on New Sarjun?"

Starla doesn't want to ask it — a yes, and it means her cousin didn't care. Or couldn't get there, but didn't bother to send a message. But she has to know if Mona knew.

There's nothing but pain in Mona's face.

"I thought you were dead, at first. Everyone thought you escaped from Redrock Prison and died in the desert."

That's the story told, that a fifteen-year-old Starla Dusai, daughter of the notorious Raj and Lasadi Dusai, ran from Redrock and perished in the Jupari Desert. But Starla assumes that most of those in the Durga System's criminal underbelly have put two and two together since a deaf teenaged girl showed up in the home of a Dusai family ally, soon after the destruction of Silk Station. Maybe that just means Mona's not a part of those gossip grapevines. A prodigal cousin of the Dusais now gone straight and narrow and out of the loop.

Though that scar says there's more to the story than straight and narrow.

"You thought I was dead at first," Starla signs.

A look of deep sadness creeps over Mona's face. "I heard, eventually. Sounded like you found a good place, like you were safe. And it's not exactly cheap to travel out here."

She could have sent a message, she could have — Starla lets it go. For now.

"Someone could recognize us here," Starla signs.

Mona wrinkles her nose. "No one who cares."

That doesn't make Starla feel any better, and she doesn't bother to keep it from her face.

"Relax." Mona grabs her drink, taps the bulb against Starla's. Sips. "I missed you," she signs when she sets the bulb back down.

Starla doesn't drink — it's never been her vice. Beads of condensation slide down the sides of her bulb, pooling in patterns that lie just out of sync with the hologrammed surface of the asteroid the table's pretending to be. The liquid seems to hover in a glossy, impossible ring.

"I missed you, too. I thought I would never find you."

"Yet you did." Mona's expression becomes cagey. "How?"

"I've been asking around Jaantzen's connections. One of them recognized you. Why are you on Maribi?"

"What kind of connections?"

Starla shrugs, rotates her wrists in midair as she tries to think of the right words. "Smugglers. People like family. No one to worry about." A thought hits her. "Are you in trouble?"

Mona shakes her head. "More the opposite."

She reaches past her own glass to take Starla's gingerly by the tip of the bulb, holds it to the minimal light. She pulls a thin tube from her pocket, telescopes it with her teeth and wands the faintly glowing internal scanner over Starla's prints.

"What are you doing?"

Mona only grins at her, hands full. After a moment, she secrets away the device and watches her comm until an ident card pops up on the screen.

"Starla Deyva," she says out loud after a moment, hands still full; the lens garbles the transcription, but Starla recognizes her alias on her cousin's expressive lips. Mona gives Starla a sad smile at the name, the first gesture that seems to jive with the sweet, timid Mona Starla used to know. "Relax," she signs. "It's slaved to my comm only."

"Do you know what happened to Deyva?" Starla asks, her fingers forming her mentor's namesign with easy memory even after so many years. But Mona only shakes her head and looks back down, absorbed by whatever she's typing into her comm.

Starla watches her, a familiar chain of thoughts slipping link by link through her mind. If Deyva had survived the attack — and that still seems less than likely, with how close to the core of

Silk Station his workshop was — he would've slipped away and remade himself in a new place, as easily as he did when he moved to Silk Station from whatever life he'd left behind that time.

And he'd tell her now to do the same.

She'd asked him once where he'd come from, and gotten nothing but a closed door in response. "The past doesn't do shit for you but tie you down," he'd told her. She'd been twelve, maybe, elbows deep in some generator he was trying to teach her to repair, so she hadn't responded. Deyva had barely understood her USL anyway.

Mona's tapping her fingers on the table beside her comm, which she's slid across the table face up. Starla's fake ident card is displayed there, along with an in-depth analysis, some of which Starla understands, most of which is coded with numbers and acronyms.

She looks up at Mona.

"Your ident card is pretty good, but there are gaps," Mona signs. "Like schooling — if someone went digging they'd see that you don't have graduation records."

Starla raises her eyebrows, thoughts of Deyva forgotten. "Just that fast?" Though she can't possibly be wanted, here in this club, the place makes her nervous. The corners are blurred, masked in holograms and dazzled by stars. There are too many things to pay attention to at once.

"No. I wrote a program to crawl for gaps. It's not standard. But I could fix them for you." Mona's expression turns mischievous. "Or I could make you a new name. It's so easy. We could disappear together. It's what I do."

"You forge identities?"

Mona shrugs. "It's just numbers in space. No looking forward. No looking backward."

Starla trails an idle thumb along her jaw, thinking. Mona's always been good at numbers, and at hiding in plain sight. Is it any surprise she might learn to hide other people, too?

Mona leans over her knees, long, thin wrists arched amid drifting constellations. Starla's caught by the intensity of her hazel eyes: they've always been flecked with gold but now the sparks are catching the neons of the strange light from the bar, like Mona's originating stars of her own, like the holograms of the bar are actually dancing lazily forth from Mona's irises.

"I don't need a new name," Starla signs. "I've already got two."

"It's not about having a new name. It's about doing it right."

"Is that how you ended up here?" Starla asks.

"I was invited," Mona signs. "People asking for help. Out here in space, it's not like if you get in trouble, you can just run until you hit a border or get off the grid. There's no way to disappear except to come see somebody like me." She smiles. "I am the border."

"Are there a lot of people looking for border crossings on Maribi?"

"Lately, it's the opposite. I was invited here by a group that plans to work against the cartel. They needed reinforcements, but most of the people they needed were on a watch list — they couldn't just waltz onto the station. And if things go badly, a lot of people on the station are going to need to get off fast. I've got them set up to do it."

A sense of unease grips Starla's stomach. What Mona is

telling her is dangerous, much more dangerous than running across Alliance troops.

"Are you saying there's going to be war?"

"The goal is for things to end cleanly," Mona signs. "But, yeah. Things could get ugly. That's why I came to find you, once I knew you were here." She leans forward. "You and me? Let's get out of here. We can go anywhere, be anyone, just like that." Mona snaps both her middle fingers, then bursts fists into stars like a magician. Glittering holograms swim in her irises.

"I can't just leave," signs Starla. "I'm here for a reason."

"On a mission for your boss?" Mona raises a skeptical eyebrow; it's clear what she thinks of the concept of bosses.

"Not just my boss, my godfather. Family."

"They're not your real family. I am."

Her words are technically true, but nothing feels farther from the truth at this moment.

"Then why didn't you try to get in touch, if you knew where I was? If you knew I was on New Sarjun — "

Mona's fingers flex, stalling for an answer. And Starla can tell she doesn't have a good one.

Starla waves a hand. "Never mind, that's not important. But you can come back home with me now, if you're tired of running."

This gets a laugh. "Running?" Mona arches an eyebrow. "I'm not running, I'm free. Be whoever I want to be, go wherever I want to go. You remember wanting that feeling? I remember you telling me how badly you wanted to leave, to go travel and see the stars. Well, that's what I'm doing. That life you always wanted? I have it, and you can have it too."

For a few seconds, Starla is transported to the past. She remembers that dream for freedom like a terrible, haunting ache deep inside. Like growing bones, period cramps. No way to ease it, impossible to ignore for long.

Mona squeezes the rest of her beer from the bulb; Starla's sits, mostly untouched. "We have a lot of catching up to do," Starla signs. "Let's not start off by fighting."

Mona's expression softens, and for a moment, behind the scar, behind the makeup, beneath the magenta hair, she looks like the timid, uncertain cousin Starla remembers.

"Come back to our hotel. I'd like you to meet Gia."

Starla almost expects her to say no, but after a brief hesitation she nods.

"I'd like that."

They begin to walk, and for a moment it almost feels like old times, elbow to elbow in the corridor, fingers flying and laughing as they catch up. It feels so much like old times that Starla nearly forgets where she is, nearly forgets the years of vigilance and training that have been drummed into her since the last time she saw her cousin.

And so the rough hand on her arm as they pass a trinket and souvenir booth catches her off guard. She tries to spin, but her attacker is stronger, and he gets his arms around her from behind.

Starla wrenches in his grasp, trying to see Mona — she's clawing at an assailant of her own.

"Run," she seems to be shouting.

But there's no way Starla is going to run.

4

GIA

L evel 15.
The Nebula.

Gia's going to find Starla there chatting, and she's going to have a calm conversation, going to be the chill big sister, not the overbearing twenty-years-older matron, the house mother.

Gia had mothers and fathers back in the commune, of course, but the authority figures she remembers the most are the brothers and sisters at Sulila, the women and men — Gia's age now — who had learned medicine well enough to teach but not to serve out their indenture in a good Sulila hospital. The most skilled were the professors. The others were house parents, eyes peeled to ensure that each new wave of incoming Sulila students adhered to the moral code: not a sip of alcohol, not a breath of smoke, not a second glance at another student's test — or body. Bots in the blood to check for intoxication. Sensors in the beds to check for . . . well.

But Gia's desire to be the chill not-a-chaperone is in a

knock-out-drag-down fistfight with the painfully dangerous reality she's lived in during the last few years of civil war.

And the panic is definitely winning.

Besides a short text an hour ago saying she was fine and not to worry, Starla has gone dark.

Gia isn't worrying, not quite. Instead, she's deflecting it into a balance of fury and barely controlled flashbacks of every time in the last three years that someone disappeared only to show up days later broken or eviscerated, like their enemies were sending her personally intricately designed puzzles to test her skills. She's counting the ones she saved and the many, many more she couldn't.

She rounds the corner of the stairwell to Level 12 — three more to go — and picks up her pace. Their enemies back home are done with. And they have no influence out here in Durga's Belt, Gia tells herself.

It doesn't help.

Level 15.

Fucking finally.

She's trying not to sprint down the corridor when she sees the commotion up ahead. Slows to reassess. She doesn't recognize three of the scrappy fighters in the mix, but she's sparred with the fourth.

Starla.

The rising panic in her chest smooths to confident assurance.

This, she can handle.

Gia wasn't looking to get in a fight, but there one is, right in front of her. Two dudes after Starla and a second girl, and

Gia doesn't need to know why or how the fight got started, she just knows they look like they need a beatdown.

And that Starla needs to stop skipping her training sessions and get her ass fit. But she'll save the I-told-you-sos for later.

The first guy has Starla from behind, pinning her arms, though his stance is off. All it would take is for Starla to drop into horse, destabilize him, jam her sharp-ass elbows into his groin.

For fuck's sake, girl. Think!

The second guy is struggling with a magenta-haired waif just about Starla's age and with the facial structure that says they share blood somewhere down the line, even if her coloring is darker, her bones finer. She's not doing any better than Starla is, though her attacker has a vicious-looking scratch down his cheek.

Girl's been fighting with her fingernails. It's not efficient, but it'll do.

The two thugs are so wrapped in their own fights that they don't see Gia until she's on them. She aims a side kick square into the knee of the man holding Starla, and is rewarded by a satisfying crunch. He goes down with a yowl, and Starla's apparently been paying enough attention to Gia's lessons that she breaks his grip and spins, driving the toe of her boot into his belly.

The other guy spots Gia, sees his buddy fall, and is fast enough to pull a knife from his belt and press it to the magenta-haired girl's throat. He edges back towards the door, footwork pulled off-balance by the squirming young woman in his grip.

"I ain't got no fight with you," he says. "Just looking for this one."

"Yeah, us too," Gia says. She hears a moan behind her, snaps in Starla's field of vision to catch her eye, points at the man on the ground. Starla may not listen to Gia normally, but at least she can take orders in a fight. She steps back to let Gia deal with the problem, her expression half determination, half terror for her cousin.

But whatever this guy's got planned for Mona, it's not killing her. Way he's holding the knife is for show — this one's got plans that need her alive.

"Stay back or I'll kill her," he bluffs, and Mona catches Gia's eye. There's only anger there, no fear. She knows he's bluffing, too.

Some of Jaantzen's crew are known for their smart talk and negotiation skills. Like Manu, he's got these quips, these little verbal pirouettes he likes to spin around before the fighting actually starts, or to head off the fighting entirely. Even Jaantzen, for all his reticence, can be a smooth talker when he wants to be.

Gia, though, is known for not dealing with assholes.

She gives Mona the faintest of nods, then strolls forward. The guy takes a step back, but Mona's dead weight and he's lost his good stance, shuffles when he realizes he's putting his back against a wall.

"Stop —"

And Gia rushes the guy. He shoves Mona out of the way to face her, but it's clear in seconds that he's not here to make a stand. He slashes wildly and Gia ducks, gets a punch to his kidney before pain lances through her upper arm.

He's gone, shoving his way past her.

Gia calms her breath, turns to make sure Starla and her cousin are all right, and finds a small crowd of gawking bystanders sprinkled along the edges of the row of shops. Knife guy may have gotten away, but the other won't be running anywhere anytime soon. He's lying in the corridor, panting and clutching the knee Gia kicked in.

"Did you enjoy the show?" Gia barks at the crowd. "Call the cops or something." Though she's not certain what passes for law enforcement on Maribi Station, and she suspects things could go just as well her way as theirs. She won't be sticking around to find out.

Her arm is throbbing, soaked with blood. She lifts her chin at the magenta-haired girl. "You better be who we've been looking for."

"I am."

"Good. Let's get the fuck out of here, then you two can tell me why you're out here getting into trouble."

Starla signs something with a roll of her eyes, and though Gia's USL is shit, she's plenty fluent in twentysomething girl.

"I don't care whose fault it is. But you're not going anywhere but the gym until we get off this rock."

"You're bleeding." This from Mona, who's grabbed a towel from somewhere and hands it to Gia. It says Maribi Station in big blue letters and has a picture of a tourist couple with cocktails in hand against a backdrop of embroidered stars.

"I noticed."

"I know this clinic, it's just a couple floors away. Non-corp clinic, non-cartel; they've fixed up a bunch of my friends for free."

"Sounds like you need better friends. And I've got plenty of credits."

Mona ignores the barb. "They're discreet," she says.

Discretion is probably a good idea at this point. People are staring, and a larger crowd is starting to gather. Someone has helped the man with the crushed knee into a chair, and Gia can't tell if it's a kindness or they're holding him for the authorities. Could go either way, on this rock, and Gia isn't going to wait to find out if she's just come down on the wrong side of a fight in a neighborhood she doesn't know.

Gia's not keen on going to a doctor she doesn't know, but she follows Mona down one corridor, then another, keeping a sharp eye behind them. No one seems to be trailing them.

"Who were those guys?" she asks. "What did they want with you?"

That flash of a look on the girl's face, she's got a lie cooking up.

"I've never seen them before in my life." She's speaking and signing as they walk, including Starla in the conversation.

"I'm sure that's true. But I bet you know what you did to piss them off."

Mona just glances over her shoulder. "We can talk about it later. We're here."

"Here" is an unassuming glass door with a snake-wrapped staff stenciled in the glass. Maribi Free Clinic is stenciled below.

There are a few others in the waiting room. Gia scans them all out of habit, but no one looks outwardly injured or sick. She's the one with blood soaking into her shirt — and it's getting looks.

"Oh my!" The woman behind the receptionist's desk looks up in alarm, then presses a button in the corner. She stands up, businesslike, and ushers Gia to a bank of seats near the door.

"It's fine," Gia tells her. "Didn't hit an artery, just needs a couple of stitches and I'll be good."

The woman makes an unconvinced noise and points at the chair again. "The doctor will be right out."

Mona and Starla are engaged in conversation, and Gia can only catch a fraction of what they're saying. She's relied too much on Starla's heads-up translator and text over the past few years rather than making the effort to learn her language. She's known that, academically. Now it's starting to sink in.

The clinic door opens and Gia looks up expecting to see a Sulila sister, maybe, or some grizzled asteroid doc. Instead she's looking straight into familiar golden eyes. Her heart stops.

For a moment, neither of them says a word. Then:

"Giaconda?"

Tevi Sharaf says her name like he doesn't quite trust his eyes, a look on his face like he's seen a ghost. And maybe he has, maybe he thought she was out of his life for good, washed his hands of her and moved on.

He doesn't much look like he's changed. A complicated cocktail of feelings swells up: regret, joy, anger.

Mostly anger.

The way he's looking to her, he doesn't seem to remember being such a shit boyfriend.

"Let's go," she says to Starla. "I've got a med kit back at the hotel."

But Tevi's already calling for a nurse like Gia's been brought in on a stretcher. Brushing away the receptionist like Gia's on death's door.

Taking her elbow to lead her back to his office like it hasn't been over twenty years since graduation day from Sulila, since he walked out of her life for good.

He's aged, but hasn't lost his good looks. Dark curls cut close and showing the first hints of salt-and-pepper, square jaw dusted with a bit of stubble, the time away from the sun — and the bad lighting in the clinic — taking a bit of the bronze out of his light-brown skin but not the spark from his golden eyes. She's staring despite herself — and despite the audience.

Starla and Mona are watching all wide-eyed like they're going to get a show.

"You and you," Gia says, stabbing a finger at each of them. "Let's go."

Starla juts her chin at Gia's bloody arm, eyebrow raised in an obvious question.

"Now."

Starla gives her a conspiratorial smile, then raises a fist to fingerspell. Gia squints in concentration, her blood-drained, Tevi-addled mind wrapping itself around the letters. *H-O* — shit, is that a *T?* — *E-L*. God, this girl must think she's daft.

"Yes," she says. "Let's go."

She realizes Tevi's still trying to get her back through the door to the examination rooms, that he's asked her the same question more than once, that he's got his scanner out and is starting to check her for a concussion, and she pulls herself together.

"Tevi, I'm fine," she snaps. She waves a hand vaguely at her arm. "Just a scratch."

He frowns at her. "There's a lot of blood for a scratch. Let me take a look."

He touches her arm, hands like they're still sharing a bed, and every fiber of her body doesn't want to stop him.

But.

No. This isn't happening.

Gia catches his wrist with her good hand, pulls him into an wristlock not hard enough to be painful but hard enough that he yelps. The scanner clatters to the floor. She forces him to his knees before releasing his hand.

"Don't touch me," she says. And in his face she sees not the anger she expected, but pain. Grief, even.

"Gia, wait."

"Fuck you," she says. She turns to leave, and when Tevi reaches to stop her, Gia doesn't bother with the ladylike slap she owes him. She decks him with a right hook and walks right back out the clinic door, ignoring the whispers, dripping blood as she goes.

5

STARLA

Gia's hotel room looks just like Starla's next door. There's a single bed and a cot that folds out, a nightstand, a single dressing bench that used to pull out of the wall but is now permanently stuck open. The bathroom is down the hall, which Starla expected from the places she'd stayed with her parents out in Durga's Belt but Gia has been complaining about.

Gia slumps onto the foot of her bed with a sigh; Starla rummages through Gia's duffel for the med kit. A thousand questions are running through her mind, but she knows better than to ask. Gia's not going to say a damn thing if she doesn't want to — their weeks together have hardly been full of heart-to-hearts, and that's even less likely now that Mona is sitting in the corner of the room.

Mona, though, has no such reservations.

"Who was the guy?" Mona asks, signing and speaking.

It earns her an expected knife-edged glare from Gia. "None of your business."

"Looked like an old boyfriend."

"Well, he wasn't a very good one."

"I've had some of those. What'd he do?"

The glare doesn't soften. Mona just lifts her hands: *All right, all right.* She pulls out her comm, entertaining herself while Starla works.

Starla sets the med kit on the edge of the bed and helps Gia out of her shirt. Gia grimaces; the fabric is already glued to her arm with a thin layer of blood. Whatever she's saying shows up in Starla's display as gibberish. Starla's really going to have to look at the language censorship setting on this thing.

The bleeding has slowed considerably and the wound doesn't look deep. Starla's honestly surprised the woman *can* bleed — sparring with her feels like punching carved obsidian. Gia lets Starla clean the wound, then takes the suture machine herself.

"Hold it there," Gia says, guiding Starla's fingers to hold the lips of the wound shut. Starla moves just ahead of the machine as Gia applies the sutures; Gia lets out another string of profanity.

"Who were those men?" Gia asks Mona. "Your own shitty old boyfriends?"

Mona doesn't look up right away, but she does stiffen, fingers still over the screen of her comm. Finally she presses a button and the screen goes dark. She slips the comm into a jacket pocket, zips it shut.

"Nothing like that," Mona says and signs.

"Seems like they had it out for you in particular."

"Not everyone on this station likes me."

"You wanna tell me why?"

Starla's trying too hard to follow the conversation and not paying enough attention to what she's doing — Gia flinches as her finger slips.

"One more," she says.

One last flash from the suture machine and the gash is a puckered caterpillar with perfectly spaced segments, an aberration in the hard topography of Gia's dark bicep. A clinic would have the tech to seal the wound in a way that would nearly eliminate the scarring, but even so, Gia's work with the suture machine is precise. Gia holds out her hand for the swab, gets to work mopping up the blood while Starla settles the suture machine into its self-sterilizer.

"I haven't been on this rock long," Gia says, dabbing at her arm. "But I get the sense it's ruled with an iron fist. Everyone says it's one of the safest places in Durga's Belt since all the crime's regulated and monopolized by one group." She drops the bloody swab into the trash chute and fixes Mona with a look. "Seems to me if someone had the gall to snatch a couple of girls in broad daylight, they weren't worried about it getting back to the cartel."

Mona shifts in her seat, crosses her arms, lower jaw jutting forward just slightly. Five years later, and she's still got the same tell Starla remembers from their childhood: she's been sniffed out.

"They were with the cartel," Starla signs, as simply as she can, and with fingerspelling for Gia's sake. "Are you in trouble?"

Mona just laughs. "In trouble?" She says the words as

she's signing. "I'm the one causing trouble. But don't worry about me — I'll be fine."

"I'm not worried about you, kid," Gia says. "I'm worried about us. Gauze?"

Starla had been about to say something, but she takes the bandage and begins to wrap Gia's arm.

"What are you mixed up with?" Gia asks.

"Why should I trust you?" Mona says and signs.

"Because your cousin does."

Mona flashes Starla a look. "Is that true?" she signs only; she's caught on that Gia's shit at USL.

Starla smooths the self-sealing end of the gauze in place. "With my life," she responds. "And with yours."

Mona finally sighs, draws her feet up onto the narrow bench to cross at the ankles, rests shoulder blades back against the metal wall behind her.

Gia shrugs on a clean shirt with a grimace of pain.

"So the cartel owns this place, right?" Mona says, fingers flying as she signs along. "And they own the crime. They set the prices for everything here: food, wages, data, oxygen, you name it."

"And tariffs and dock fees," Gia says.

"Absolutely. Workers here aren't indentured, but they might as well be — they can't negotiate their salaries, they work shitty hours and like it, they don't get any medical care. You saw that charity clinic where your old boyfriend works."

Mona winks at Gia, and to Starla's astonishment, Gia doesn't look pissed at her for the needling.

"You want a better job, what can you do?" Mona says and signs. "Work for someone else? There is no one else. You complain, you try to organize for your rights, and you get tossed out an airlock." Mona gives Gia a pointed look. "The cartel doesn't allow collective bargaining — unless it's coming from rich trading partners like your boss. And even then, we'll see how far you get."

It's an odd way of phrasing it, but it is what Jaantzen and Julieta Yang and all the others are doing with this meeting, isn't it? Collective bargaining.

"What does this all have to do with you?" Gia asks.

"People are tired of it," Mona says. "The dockworkers and some of the other workers on the station, they've formed an underground union to organize themselves, and they're going to force the cartel to listen." She smiles, and there's a spark of danger in it that Starla doesn't recognize. "Even if it means forcing them out."

"When."

"I don't know." Mona shrugs, and Starla can't tell if she truly doesn't. This new creature in front of her is so close to the cousin she remembers, yet so foreign. "That's not my part in it," Mona says.

"Your part is to forge identities," Starla signs.

"Yes, my part is making false identities." Mona's seen Gia's look of fierce concentration at Starla's USL and is falling back into her childhood role of interpreter. "I did up the ident cards that got the mercenaries they need onto this station, and the ones that will help the organizers escape if they need to when everything goes down. And I plan to be long gone before that happens."

"Then you better get out of here soon," Gia says.

"What do you mean?" Starla asks.

"I mean I was approached today by someone claiming to represent a group planning to overthrow the cartel," Gia says. "He wanted to offer Jaantzen a better deal, and said we needed to act before tomorrow's meeting."

Mona takes a long, slow breath. "I would take that offer. I've seen the firepower these guys have built up. There's no way the cartel knows it's coming." Mona unfolds herself from the narrow dressing bench and stands. "I have one last bit of work to do before I'm free to go. Sounds like I should probably take care of that." She pulls out her comm and opens a new message, begins to type.

"I'll go too," Starla signs.

Gia's eyebrows shoot up. "Over my dead body are you two heading back out there alone. First there's Alliance troops, now you get jumped in broad daylight — or whatever you call this — and you think I'll just let you go?"

"I'll be careful," Starla signs, but Gia doesn't seem to understand, so she pulls out her comm and begins to type.

I'll be careful, Starla types. *We were talking. We'll pay better attention.*

"Damn right you'll pay better attention," says Gia.

And maybe her paranoia is justified, but there's no way Starla's going to sit in her dingy little hotel room while her newly found cousin disappears again.

Gia's said something Starla missed, the words blinking on and off the heads-up display. Starla holds up a finger. *Listen*, she types. *And don't say anything yet.*

She shows the screen to Gia, gets a nod of agreement.

I trust Mona not to harm me. I don't know who her friends are, but we need information, don't we?

Gia's lips quirk to the side; it's reluctant assent. Starla holds up her finger again before she can answer.

I'LL GO ASK QUESTIONS, I'LL COME RIGHT BACK. MONA WILL TELL ME MORE WITH YOU NOT AROUND.

But Gia just shakes her head.

YOU'RE NOT MY BABYSITTER.

"You try telling Jaantzen that."

Starla has no doubts that Jaantzen gave Gia strict orders to keep her out of trouble, but what? She's going to tie her up? Knock her out? Lock her in her room?

I'M GOING WITH MY COUSIN. I'M SORRY.

Gia holds her gaze for three breaths, then sighs deeply. "Fine," she says. "Just keep in touch so I know where you are, and don't stay long. And watch your back."

I DON'T NEED YOU TO TELL ME TO WATCH MY BACK.

"I don't care what you think you need. What do you think your godfather does to me if I come home without you?"

Starla starts to type, Nothing, he's not a monster — Gia's being ridiculous and Jaantzen certainly wouldn't blame her for Starla's choices. But Gia just waves a hand.

"Forget him. I would never forgive myself. And he would never forgive himself for not coming with us." For a moment, something raw and emotional slips through the cracks of Gia's fierce expression. She tamps it back down before Starla can guess at what it means. "Just promise me you won't do anything stupid."

"Fine," Starla signs. "I promise."

"That had better mean what I hope it meant," Gia says. "I know you're an adult and I'm not a babysitter, but I am your friend. And we're both in an unfamiliar place. Just do me a favor, okay?"

Starla nods. DON'T PUNCH ANY OTHER DOCTORS WHILE I'M GONE, she types, testing a little joke and emboldened by the way Mona seems to have escaped unscathed from Gia's prickly lack of humor.

It gets her a wry little smile, then Gia claps her shoulder.

"Go be safe," she signs — or tries to sign.

Starla understands her anyway.

6

GIA

The best cure for the burning ache of a knife wound is probably sleep, but Gia still has work to do tonight. Fortunately, there's a run-down little watering hole just down the corridor from the hotel, and a drink could just be the next best thing.

Gia settles into a spot at the far end of the bar where her back's to the wall and she can see the door, then scrolls through her messages. One from Calanthe Yang finalizing details for the meeting tomorrow. One from the medtech she left in charge back in Bulari, updating her on the status of the human rubble left in the wake of the war. She scrolls through until she finds the name she wants.

MANU JURIC: NO SIGNIFICANT IMPROVEMENT.

A hot stab of disappointment pierces her gut. She downs the rest of her beer, orders another. Opens a message to tell Jaantzen about Lorn's offer, and that Starla's made contact with Mona.

She doesn't tell him the more worrisome bits of this trip — he's got enough on his plate at the moment without hearing about knife fights, or that Starla's currently out adventuring.

Gia's trying not to worry about her. The first argument that surfaces in favor of not worrying is that Gia was Starla's age when she was shipped off to prison — and she survived just fine. It's an argument that would be more compelling if not immediately followed by memories of just how naive young Gia was at the time, how little prepared to handle what had been about to happen.

It's been almost twenty years since she ended up in Redrock Prison, Gia realizes. She's reached the point where more than half her life has happened on the other side of ruin. There's no tipping *that* scale back. No going back to the girl she remembers being: sunny and hopeful, a newly minted doctor ready to make a real difference in the world.

She'd been born in the New Sarjunian desert to a commune of religious types who believed in everything and nothing, two parts superstition and one part mysticism. A lot of "seize your destiny" talk, but she'd bridled at the way they closed themselves off from people who actually needed their help. We could be doing more, she would say — only to be told, We can't save everyone, so why try?

She signed up for Sulila in an act of rebellion. It was a corporate university. It was religious, but offered a profession she could actually use to do good in the world, even if it meant indenturing herself to get that education.

She and Tevi Sharaf had graduated together and had both gotten indenture offers at a Sulila hospital in the Fingers —

the slums in the ravines east of Bulari. It was even more run-down then than it is today, with more bodies showing up on the street than even in the past few years of civil war. The culprit in those days and in the war was one and the same: a young and vicious woman who called herself Blackheart and was dedicated to shredding her way to the top of the streets.

Gia had stitched wounds, set bones, pulled out bullets, but none of it made a difference. She was mopping blood out of an arterial wound, and no one was doing anything to stop the bleeding at the source.

There's nothing we can do about it, that was Tevi's argu-ment during those long nights when she'd rail to him about the injustice of it all. We're doctors, not the police, he would say. We're doing all we can.

But one day, when Gia couldn't save one too many kids, she found herself holding a child's mother as she wept. And she learned that it was common knowledge who the killer was, even though the police were telling her over and over they couldn't find the perpetrators.

She coaxed evidence from the mother and took it to a detective she thought she could trust, and was relieved when they actually arrested the guy.

Tevi warned her she was playing with fire, but Gia became obsessed with learning everything she could about Blackheart's crew, gathering evidence from her patients, passing it along to the police. Information was her power: making connections, gaining trust, making a difference.

At least, until Blackheart identified the star confidential informant who was testifying against some of her most powerful lieutenants and turned the tables, framing Gia so perfectly that even her closest friends — even her lover — shook their heads like *We can't believe we never knew her* as she was shipped off to Redrock.

Fuck them, anyway.

Gia is nearly finished with her second glass of the diesel-fumed local buzz when the door to the watering hole swings open and the last person she wanted to find on this station steps inside.

Tevi's changed out of his scrubs and is wearing a simple pair of gray slacks that fit him very well and a ribbed black sweater with sleeves pushed up his toned forearms. A delicate gold Sulila ID bracelet circles his right wrist like a shackle. He's shaved off the afternoon's stubble, and outside the harsh light of the clinic waiting room, she can't see the salting of silver in his curls.

He looks exactly like she remembers.

Gia's light-headed from blood loss and booze, but she's off her stool with her hand on her weapon before he steps another foot towards the bar.

The bartender glances between them, remembers some more pressing matter in the back room.

"Giaconda." Tevi's voice is soft, melodic. "Can we talk?"

"Rather not."

"C'mon." He takes a slow step towards her, then another, and when she doesn't react to that, he closes the distance between them and slips onto the bar stool beside her. Slowly, like he's sidling up to a stray he's not sure won't bite.

Won't bite again, at least. He's cleaned himself up, but a

lump mars his fine jawline, flushed dark under his golden-brown skin.

Gia wants to feel satisfied by that. She doesn't.

But she sits back down and thumbs her comm back on to finish the message to Jaantzen. Buying herself time.

Apparently reassured by the lack of an all-out fight in his bar, the bartender warily returns from the back room and comes over to greet his new guest. Tevi orders two of something Gia's never heard of; it sounds healthy, not intoxicating, and when it shows up she sniffs it suspiciously. It smells like vinegar and lavender. It reminds her of rancid bath soap.

Tevi taps his glass against her untouched one and sips a bit of the froth off the top, his tongue darting out to catch the smudge of foam that remains on his upper lip.

"I hope I'm not intruding," he says.

"Hope springs eternal."

"I just wanted to apologize."

Even in her light-headedness, Gia remembers to bite her tongue. The best way to scuttle a well-meant apology is to be a bitch about it. She reaches for the new drink in front of her for something to do with her hands. It tastes astringent and faintly sweet — way better than it smells.

"I deserved that punch," Tevi says. "If you want to know the truth, I've been wanting somebody to punch me for what I did to you for years."

Gia spares him a glance; he's staring at his drink. "I'll do it again if you need me to," she says. She's rewarded by the twitch of a smile on the corner of his lips.

"I couldn't believe my eyes when you walked in today," he

says. "It was like, all these years I've been wanting to apologize, and I haven't even known how to get started finding you."

Gia doesn't trust herself to answer. She takes another sip of the vinegar-soap drink instead.

"'You could save a lot more lives with a gun than with a med kit,'" Tevi quotes, and the skin between Gia's shoulder blades prickles with memory. "Do you remember saying that?"

She does. In her mind's eye they're hiking, one of their rare days off together, an early morning hike before the sun's blasting down. Gia used to love hiking — the loneliness, the empty sky, the birds, the fauna and flora, everything that used to be within arm's length growing up. These days, the desert just reminds her of Redrock, of days battling thirst and heat and exhaustion, hard labor, sand everywhere and nowhere to wash it off, scorpions lurking in her boots and in the corners of her cell.

Now she hates leaving the city. But that day, they'd stopped at a vantage point in the bluffs above Bulari. They were to the north of the city, the valley below them a glittering mess of skyscrapers in the downtown core that flattened out in all directions to sprawl into the plains. The bluff they were standing on wraps around to the southeast, the five ravine slums of Bulari clawing into the hills like fingers. From so high up, you couldn't see the carnage happening where the second and third finger joined, where Blackheart's territory disputes were filling their hospital with bodies.

When Gia remembers that day, she remembers wishing she could enjoy the scenery, but only being able to stare in rage at the spot she'd left, knowing that when she returned that afternoon, more would be dead.

It was one of the last times they had truly spent together. After all those nights staying up smoking and drinking while she fumed about the indenture system, growing increasingly obsessed with the kids in the emergency rooms, in hunting down the monsters who were doing this to them — they'd grown apart. Gia was finding solace in her quest, and Tevi cautioned that she was going outside the bounds of her oath with all this talk of vengeance.

This talk of saving more lives with a gun than with a med kit.

"Yeah, I remember saying that."

She's not sure if she believes it now, or if now she just understands that there are always more killers hiding behind the ones you take out.

Maybe some force brings more order. Maybe the Maribi Cartel, for example, has a low body count because they run a tight ship. Maybe a Bulari with her boss Jaantzen in charge and Blackheart gone is a safer place, or maybe it's just become unsafe for a different set of people — she doesn't know.

She's not a philosopher, she's a fighter.

"What are you doing on this rock?" she asks. She juts a chin at the chain on his wrist. "You still working for Sulila?"

"Yeah. This clinic isn't a Sulila one, it's run by a local charity. Some of the people coming into Maribi haven't seen a doctor in years. They come in, get fixed up, ship back out into the black. The clinic's model's good, though — they train locals in Durga's Belt for free in exchange for a commitment to work for two years at the clinic before finding other work."

She frowns. "Still sounds like an indenture."

He shakes his head. "No contracts, just the honor system. We've got some doctors who've been there over a decade. Others go back to their home stations and start their own practices. Others go get good jobs on one of the planets, or take on with a ship's crew. It's providing well-paying jobs and much-needed medical personnel out here."

"We could use something like that on New Sarjun."

"I've been thinking about that," he says. He's starting to relax, that spark glinting in his eye as he shares his dream. "I'm here on loan from Sulila to help with training, but I also needed to get away and think about what's next for me. I earned out my indenture five years ago and I don't have family tying me down, so I think it's time for a change."

Gia makes a noncommittal noise, realizing too late that it sounds dismissive. The truth is, listening to Tevi's optimism and plans to make a difference in the future is putting an uncomfortable twist in her gut.

Or maybe it's the vinegar-soap drink, which she pushes away.

Or maybe it's annoyance at the giddy flip in her stomach when he said "no family tying me down."

"You look good," Tevi finally says, and instantly a flush creeps into his cheeks. "Fit. I mean, you obviously are fit." He rubs a palm over his jaw where she hit him with a rueful smile. "You train?"

"As much as I can."

"And how's life? Still on New Sarjun? Kids? Married?" He gives her a too-casual smile at that last question, then clears his throat.

"Just to my job."

"And what is it you do?"

"Right now? Manage shipping logistics for a small Bulari importer." It's true enough this week; what she does for Jaantzen changes day by day.

"That sounds uneventful." Another look, this time pointedly, at the bulk of bandage visible under the thin silhouette of her sleeve. "Did you get in a fight with a shipping AI?"

"Muggers." Gia takes a long drink of her beer.

"That doesn't happen on Maribi. The people in charge — "

"Keep it safe. I've heard the propaganda."

He glances around, but she didn't say it loud.

"Well, it sounds interesting," he says, though it clearly doesn't. Gia's fully aware of how gamely he's trying to engage her in conversation, and how difficult she's making it. She just hasn't decided yet if she's ready to play along.

This trip to Maribi Station was supposed to be a cakewalk to help take her mind off what's been going on back home — not a meet-and-greet with old ghosts.

She tips back the rest of her beer, shakes her head when the bartender catches her eye. Having another tonight isn't going to make anything better. The only thing that will is heading back to her hotel room and burying herself in work until she falls asleep.

"Giaconda."

She's breathing shallow. Nobody says her name like that. Not anymore.

"Gia, what happened to you?"

Gia shifts in her stool to look at him full, considering.

What happened to her? It's written on her body in tattoos any asshole can see.

"Prison," she says.

"I can see where you've been," he says. "I asked what happened to you."

Coming out of any other mouth, Gia would've left right then and there. Coming out of Tevi's, the question's filled with genuine curiosity and compassion. He always did have that way of making you want to bare your soul, tell him your truths because no one else in the world seemed to actually care when they asked. She's seen complete strangers open up to Tevi, tears streaming down their faces as they answer his question, "Tell me how you're doing," with more honesty than they've answered anything in years.

It's a heady feeling, being seen, and for a moment all Gia feels is lightness, yearning, an overwhelming desire to share her story with the one person who will truly listen.

What happened to her?

"Long story," she says, and because old habits die hard, because her old instinct is still to derail his intense emotional gaze into safer, less vulnerable territory, she finds herself saying, "But I got a few tattoos in more interesting places I could show you."

She sees the way his pulse quickens, the Adam's apple jump in his throat. And maybe she'd only meant that as a joke, but heat is blooming in her belly now.

His smooth fingers find hers, his golden brown against her midnight black. Stars are born in the places their skin touches, scattering deliciously through her nervous system.

"Gia," Tevi says softly. "I'm so sorry I didn't believe you."

There's a flood of pain hiding behind the barrier that will fall if she allows herself to contemplate the sincerity of his apology.

So she doesn't. She leans against the back of the bar stool, fingers still laced in his, and lifts an eyebrow. "Then why don't we go someplace where you make it up to me?" she asks.

And she doesn't even regret it.

7

STARLA

Starla's been feeling like she has a handle on Maribi Station's layout, but Mona slips through it like she grew up here. She leads them through secret corridors and service entrances, and twice she gives a subtle sign to a rough-looking worker who lets them through an entrance he's casually pretending not to guard.

The longer Starla's on Maribi, the less it's starting to feel like home. Nothing on Silk Station was really off-limits other than someone else's quarters. Nothing needed to be guarded because there were no secrets — there was only the wild, tangled nest of the extended Dusai clan.

Their destination is a door, half-hidden behind the slumped husk of a forklift suit. The suit is missing an arm, and it looks like most of the wiring has been salvaged — nobody's going to come looking for it anytime soon. Mona raps on the door in a precise pattern, and after a moment the handle turns and juts forward an inch. Mona pulls the door open and motions Starla through.

The room beyond is cramped and hot, shot through with the vibrating hum of servers, glowing with monitors, and draped with a spider's web of wiring and cables. A guy about their age is absorbed in a screen — he glances up long enough to see Mona beside Starla, then holds up a finger and goes back to what he's doing. His skin is a rich dark brown, his cloud of black hair cut short and teased into a sea of spikes, concentration held in his pointed chin. He's wearing what looks like a dockworker's jumpsuit, with a prosthetic glove encasing his right hand.

Starla leans in for a closer look. The prosthetic's a cage of tendons and pulleys designed to compensate for his partially missing middle three fingers. The exoskeleton fits snugly over the back of his hand, but the ring finger seems to be off — the boy taps it against the table every few keystrokes in an attempt to straighten it back out, but it doesn't seem to be slowing his typing any. He's got a rhythm.

"This is Ahmed," Mona signs, speaking aloud to include Ahmed; he doesn't get a namesign. "Ahmed, this is Starla."

Ahmed lifts his chin but doesn't look away from his work. "Hey, Starla," he says, the words scrolling across her lens. "Gimme a second."

Mona pushes a stool towards her and finds her own perch on the open corner of a table. Starla watches Ahmed's screen, but she can't tell what he's doing. She's always had an intuitive sense of how machines work mechanically, but the intangible flow of numbers and information within a computer is not her thing.

Ahmed's back is to them, so Starla figures they can talk without disrupting his concentration.

"Who is Ahmed?" Starla signs, and the twinkle in Mona's eye tells her before her cousin's hands can make the sign.

"A friend," she signs, though the mischievous dimple in her cheek says he's clearly more. "He works for the Dockworkers Union."

"What's he working on?" Starla asks.

"The last few false identities for union workers. They're pretty confident they can win if the cartel tries to break their strike, but they need an out in case something goes wrong."

Mona looks over Ahmed's shoulder, cheek brushing cheek, and says something to him that comes through as technical garbage on Starla's heads-up display; he nods and goes back a few lines of code, replaces a few characters.

"I've been doing this for longer, but he's almost as good as me now," Mona signs in explanation. She winks. "Almost."

"How'd you learn?"

"Do you have all night?" Mona asks with an expression that says, *It's a long story.*

"I have all the time you want."

"Well . . ."

All the rust has shaken off Mona's USL since their first few moments in the Nebula. Now her hands are fluid as mercury, her expression shifting from guarded to open, even silly at times, as she launches into a story about bouncing around the Belt with the few cousins she'd escaped with, reuniting briefly with her older brother Amit before he wandered on to his next big adventure. About ending up in a public boarding school for orphans and children of deep space crew members on one of Indira's moons before she learned the intricacies of creating new fingerprints, new names, new lives.

About slipping out of the boarding school with no money, just a clutch of stolen ident cards which helped her open bank accounts, about the years of learning the subtle ways to dance through the back webs of financial institutions without getting caught, about starting to make a name for herself as the person to go to if you needed to disappear.

"And that's just your life, now?" Starla asks. "Disappearing?"

"It's worked this long, hasn't it?" Mona glances over Ahmed's shoulder again; he's still busily typing. "Tell me about New Sarjun. Do you like it?"

And so Starla tells her about the planet she's started to think of as home. At first it's benign things, about the heat, the incessant grit, the sandstorms that blacken the horizon and clog the air filters, what it's like to see a moon through atmosphere, to see Indira on the horizon, to have Durga so bright.

She stays light and Mona doesn't probe. Starla's still not sure how to talk about the things that have truly passed since she last saw her cousin. Her parents' deaths, what it was like in the Alliance prison before Jaantzen broke her out, how lonely she is even among friends.

"I'm done," Ahmed says, and Starla breaks away from the small talk with relief. Ahmed spins the chair around to face them, rolling his neck and taking the prosthetic glove off with a sigh — she can see places where calluses have built up on his knuckles, the scarring around his wrist where the harness clamps on awkwardly.

"Can I look at it?" Starla signs, glad for another topic besides the one which was starting to hit too close for comfort. "I might be able to fix the finger."

"Yeah, let Starla look at it!" Mona's speaking as she signs again; she holds out her hands to take it from Ahmed and pass it to Starla. "She's amazing with machines."

Starla holds up a hand, raises an eyebrow, like *Don't over-sell me*. But the problem is apparent instantly. One of the pins in the fingertip's hinge is too short and worn round by use, allowing the bracket to shift off the pin and bind up. It needs a new pin — or, maybe she can fix it with the length of wire coiled on the table beside her.

"Do you have a tool kit?" she asks Mona, who rummages for one on the crowded table behind her.

A few moments later, Starla hands the prosthetic back. Ahmed flips the cage back over his hand. He flexes his fingers, turns back to the terminal and types. His face lights up with a grin.

"That's perfect, thanks!" He runs through his fingers a few more times, then undoes the prosthetic again. "Work acci-dent," he says. "I managed to cobble this thing together with the help of some friends and some free printer plans I found on the net, but the cartel doesn't really pay out wages if you hurt yourself and can't work. Meant I had plenty of time to learn skills that don't involve being on the wrong end of a ten-ton shipping crate being pushed through zero G. You may float like nothing else, but a shipping crate still feels like ten tons when it hits your fingers."

Mona's watching her to see how much she's caught, and Starla gives her a thumbs up. The heads-up unit's transcription software doesn't always work with strange accents, but either Ahmed's is pretty close to standard New Sarjunian or he's speaking clearly enough for the tech to catch almost everything.

"Did you finish what we needed to?" Mona asks him.

Ahmed nods. "You should check it over, but I think we're good to go." He gets up, stretching carefully in the cramped space so he doesn't hit anyone. Mona takes his chair and leans into the screen, scrolling through the lines of text.

"Mona tells me you're here as part of that group that's trying to negotiate better terms with the cartel," Ahmed says. He's half turned away from her now, one eye on what Mona's doing, making it harder for Starla to verify what the display's telling her with what his lips seem to be saying.

YOU KNOW ABOUT THAT? Stella types on her comm. She shows him the screen and he laughs.

"Of course. Everyone in the union thinks it's hilarious to see a bunch of off-worlders thinking they can come and negotiate with the cartel. Clearly none of you have tried to before." His expression grows darker. "It doesn't work."

BUT THEY ALLOW UNIONS? Starla types. I DIDN'T THINK THEY DID.

"Of course not. If they get even a whiff of what we're up to, we're all out an airlock. And they're starting to get suspicious, which is why it's time to act. They're getting close to figuring out who we are. Especially — " He gives Mona a concerned look, and whatever he says next is too muffled, his face turned away.

"It'll be fine. Did you get the stuff I asked you for?" Mona says.

He answers and she turns back to the screen. They're both turned away from Starla now, and Starla can feel the electric hum of the room in her chest. It must be dampening their voices, because only a few scant words push through to fracture in her heads-up display. She switches it off and entertains herself tracing wires from machine to machine, matching what she sees with systems configurations she's been studying lately.

Mona scritches her nails above Starla's elbow to get her attention, a gesture unchanged by the years. On the screen behind her, data is streaming from one server to another.

"We're good to go," she signs. Then, speaking to Ahmed: "Tell Berzac the file's encrypted and I'll send him the code as soon as I'm off this rock."

Starla doesn't miss the glance shared between them. There's something deeper behind it on Ahmed's end: pain, resolve, reluctance, disappointment.

Mona stands, breaking eye contact with him sharply; Ahmed's gaze lingers a moment longer before he picks up his prosthetic and begins to test the finger, as though trying to distract himself.

Mona turns to Starla with a smile. "I hope you're as good with scissors as you are with a screwdriver," she signs.

Starla raises her eyebrows. If Mona is looking for a craft partner, she's going to be disappointed. "That's a solid no."

But Mona just flicks a wrist dismissively. "You'll do just fine."

The apartment Ahmed and Mona are sharing is little bigger than the hotel rooms Gia and Starla are in. The bed's a little wider, and there's room for a chair as well as a dressing bench, along with a tiny pull-down counter in the kitchenette and a rehydrator that looks barely big enough to fit a single ration box.

Mona goes immediately to the bed, roots through the shopping bag sitting there. "This is perfect, baby," she says to Ahmed; he's drifted in the door behind them. She pulls out a pair of scissors, a comb, a couple of bottles labeled things like Creme Developer and (Into The) Black.

While Mona's busy setting out bottles, Starla takes the opportunity to text Gia: AT MONA'S PLACE I'M FINE. BE HOME SOON.

After a moment she gets the reply.

I'M OUT. MESSAGE ME WHEN YOU'RE HOME.

Out? Grabbing a drink? Starla doesn't think Gia has any friends here, unless . . .

Mona's gentle nails on Starla's arm get her attention. "What's up?" Mona signs.

Starla shows her the comm. "I wonder who she's out with."

Mona claps her hands in delight. "That doctor! God, he was hot." It's a sign Starla hasn't seen in years, their own personal slang for the dreamy vid stars they used to fawn over as girls. It brings with it a stab of longing; Starla shoves the feeling aside.

Starla throws up her eyebrows in mock horror. "He was ancient!"

"Oh, honey." Mona gives her a secret smile. "Old and experienced is a good thing. Here."

Mona hands Starla the scissors, then shucks off her chunky knit sweater. Beneath the bulky garment she's scrawny, shoulder blades jutting like knives.

"I'm thinking short in the back and long in the front," Mona signs; she's voicing again, too. Starla glances over to where Ahmed has been watching them sign, curious. "But we can just play with it until we come up with something that seems to work. I've never had short hair, it's probably going to be a mess with my curls." She frowns at Starla. "Do you think I should just straighten it? I hadn't thought about that."

Starla shrugs, shares a look with Ahmed. Fashion isn't her strong point, and she's never cut anyone's hair before. She sets the scissors down. "I don't know what will look good," she signs. "What are you going for?"

"Different," Mona says and signs; Starla catches Ahmed's wince. Mona hands Starla her comm, with an ident card displayed. Rania Jacovsin, it reads. There's a list of demographic stats, but no photo. "Make me look like somebody who has this name, whoever she is."

Tentatively at first, then with gusto at the sharp, tactile feel of the blades through Mona's thick hair, Starla starts to cut. Swaths of magenta curls coil on the floor at her feet.

She catches Ahmed's expression in the mirror; he looks physically pained, though he hasn't said a word. After the first few cuts, he leaves, with a comment about the room being too crowded, and Mona's shoulders finally relax when he's gone. She breathes out, slow.

Stella catches her eye in the mirror and lifts an eyebrow: *You gonna tell me or what?*

"He doesn't want me to go," Mona signs. "But what will I do here? Sure, I think his union can win, especially given what I've seen of the cartel. But I'm not gonna risk being here if they don't. And even if they do, I'm done with this place. Time for something new."

Starla takes the opportunity to set the scissors down and fluff Mona's hair before she answers. "He doesn't want to go with you?"

Mona shakes her head. "He keeps saying he'll come maybe later, but we both know he's not really going to. He's invested in this place, in this fight. That's just not me."

"And who are you?"

"Rania Jacovsin," Mona fingerspells. "Or whoever."

"Come back to New Sarjun. You can be whoever you want to be there."

"No I can't. There I'm your cousin."

"You're my cousin no matter where you are."

Mona gives an annoyed little shake of her head. "You know what I mean. This looks good." She rakes her fingers through her new bob.

Starla manages to keep the conversation away from heated topics while they pull the magenta dye from Mona's curls, rinsing her hair in the tiny bathroom sink before daubing (Into The) Black in its place.

But she can't help thinking she should have been there when Mona dyed the magenta in the first place, that she should have been there through whatever gave her that scar down her cheek. That they never should have been separated.

"What is it?" Mona asks, when they've got her dye-soaked hair safely wrapped and have rinsed most of the traces of purplish-black from their hands.

Starla flexes her hands, thinking how to phrase it. "I'm just thinking about how much we missed," she signs finally.

She's said the wrong thing; Mona's face closes down.

"Why do you spend so much time thinking about the past," Mona signs. "Here's a tip: Don't obsess about it, and you'll be happier."

Starla frowns at her. "What's so wrong with thinking about happy times?"

"Don't you get it?" Mona says out loud; Starla's touched a nerve to get Mona to forget to sign. Mona glances at the door as though she'd been louder than she intended, then switches back to sign. "Silk Station is gone," she continues. "Your parents are dead. My mother is dead. Everyone we know is dead and gone."

"Not everyone."

"Does it matter?" Mona pauses, and a muscle twitches and sets in her jaw. Starla can see her resolve stiffen, her spine straighten. "I don't think about the past," Mona signs. "I learned not to at the boarding school. You think about the good times and you just get sad. You think about how your family's all dead, and you start to cry. You think about the last thing you ever said to your brother, and it's devastating because you don't know if you'll ever see him again."

And the resolve softens, just a touch, just enough for Starla to rub a tentative thumb across Mona's knee.

"I know," Starla signs. "Of course I know."

"How did you deal with it?" Mona asks.

Starla shrugs. "I was angry. But I decided I needed to find everyone. I had a goal."

Mona stiffens again as though rebuked.

Shit. "I didn't mean — "

"I thought you were dead." Mona voices the words as she signs, snarls it, teeth bared and defensive.

"I didn't mean you weren't looking for me."

"I thought you were dead," Mona signs again, but this time it's not an excuse, it's grief.

Starla pulls her into her arms. She can feel the vibrations of Mona's vocal cords humming against her shoulder, feel her soft, hot breath on her neck, but she can't see Mona's lips, and if her heads-up display transcribes whatever it is Mona is saying, Starla can't tell — it's fogged from tears that have appeared from nowhere.

Mona stinks of sharp, astringent hair chemicals and old cigarette smoke.

Starla circles *sorry* over her heart, in front of Mona's nose, and Mona nods into her collarbone, hands clawed into the back of Starla's shirt.

Eventually Starla breaks the embrace, releasing Mona and feeling her cousin's hands go slack, the muscles which had been like iron bands melting back into flesh, and fall to her side. Mona rubs the back of her hand across her eyes — they're red-rimmed now, her makeup has smeared, and she suddenly seems so much younger. The gangly teenager Starla remembers, not this poised and angry young woman Starla doesn't know what to do with.

Mona turns back to the mirror and daubs at her face with a towel, blotting away streaks of eyeliner, though not the signs of her grief. Her shoulders finally slump into stillness, and her body relaxes, leaning to rest against Starla's comfortably.

"I should leave this in another hour," she finally signs, wafting open hands at her wrapped hair. "And you should probably go home before your bodyguard gets done with her booty call."

Starla lets herself laugh at that.

"How do I get in touch with you?" she asks, seriously.

Mona grabs Starla's comm and types her number in, followed by another, more complicated address. "That's my local comm, I'll have it while I'm on Maribi. But you can always call me at that other address. No one knows that one and I can check it anywhere."

They hug again, and this time it's fierce.

"I'll see you before you or I go," Mona signs. "I promise."

8

GIA

A chime from her comm — the "it's the boss" chime — wakes her.

It takes her a moment to realize that she was dreaming, because she never sleeps deeply enough to dream; it takes a moment longer to realize she's not in her Bulari apartment — or in her hotel bed on Maribi. Or alone.

She blinks herself awake with heart racing to find Tevi. Okay. She checks the time on her comm: it's still plenty early. Good.

A new message from Jaantzen blinks on the screen. Gia rolls away from Tevi's gentle snores, then plays the message with the volume almost all the way down.

A trick of the camera is painting Jaantzen's dark-brown skin ashen, and he's thinner than she's ever seen him. Not gaunt — the big man will never be gaunt. But . . . haunted.

She glances over her shoulder as the message begins to play, but Tevi doesn't wake. Twenty years later and the man can still sleep through anything, bolstered by a babe-like innocence and trust.

It continues to be maddening.

"Thank you for letting me know about the potential counteroffer," Jaantzen says. "I find it compelling, but I trust your judgment on the ground. Ah, so to speak." He rubs a palm absently over the back of his neck, thinking; he looks exhausted. Gia finds herself simultaneously wishing she was there to help and guiltily grateful to be far from it all.

"My gut says yes," he finally says. "But talk with Ms. Yang before making a final decision. Follow her lead."

It's what Gia would've done if she hadn't been able to reach Jaantzen. Calanthe Yang and her mother have more experience with international shipping matters than Jaantzen does — and certainly more than Gia does.

Jaantzen clears his throat. "I'll make the funds available to you if you need them. And give my . . . regards to Starla." He leans forward to switch off the screen.

"Do whatever the Yangs do, tell Starla you love her," Gia mutters, translating.

Beside her, Tevi stirs. "Who was that?" He yawns.

"My boss."

Gia switches the screen off; Jaantzen's face and name gets around New Sarjun, especially lately, but there's no reason Tevi should recognize his voice. She feels another twinge of guilt at wanting to hide who she works for. Everyone she knows now in Bulari is aware she works for one of the more notorious crime bosses in the city, and for years, being one of Willem Jaantzen's people has been a badge of honor.

But the thought of telling Tevi gives her pause, and that pause fills her with shame.

Though what does it matter? She'll be off this rock and never see him again after this.

She tosses her comm onto her balled-up pile of clothes and rolls back to face him. Tevi's all pecs and sleep-tousled curls in a tangle of sheets. He gives her a smile that erases twenty years and makes her heart stop beating.

"I gotta work," she says. She doesn't have a lot of experience ending these sorts of things. "Thanks."

"And I should get back to the clinic," he says, but his smile doesn't fade. She'd meant it as a farewell, but apparently he isn't taking it that way. "Maybe we can meet for dinner tonight?"

"Maybe," she says, managing to make her tone sharp even though her words betrayed her. Tevi's smile fades.

"Let me take a look at your arm before you go, at least," he says. The sheets slide down as he sits up; she cuts her gaze quickly away.

But she stays a moment longer, lets him unwind the bandage and reapply the dressing in silence. He doesn't tell her she should come into the clinic and have him fix it up so it doesn't scar; he knows she knows.

He finishes and she shrugs her shirt on, grateful for the thin layer of clothing between her skin and his touch. She busies herself finding the rest of her scattered garments and putting herself back together.

"How do I find you again?" he asks. When she looks back, he's pulled on his scrubs; she relaxes a fraction more.

"Give me your number," she says, a slip of the tongue —

what is wrong with her? She tells herself to mistype it, to forget it, but her fingers ignore her and type the correct number into her comm as he speaks.

"My post ends in three months," he says. "Then I'll be back on New Sarjun. I'd like to see you again."

"I'll call you," she says before she means to. For fuck's sake.

She can't call him. Their paths diverged decades ago, and she can't see a way to bridge that gap back into his world.

No. This has to be it.

She realizes she's lingering awkwardly, waiting. That he is, too. A couple of hours ago, being tangled together in sheets and nothing else had felt like the most natural thing in the world; now, she won't be comfortable around him unless they're both chastely zipped into vac suits.

She takes a step towards the door before she realizes he's still holding her hand. Or is she holding his?

For a moment she thinks he'll kiss her, but he doesn't try. Tevi just squeezes her hand and steps back.

———

She almost manages to sneak into the shower cubicle in the hallway outside her hotel room, but Starla's door opens just as Gia is keying in. It might look like a regular morning trip to shower, or it might look like Gia's still wearing yesterday's clothes and didn't make it to her own bed last night.

From the conspiratorial look Starla gives her, Gia's pretty sure it looks like the latter.

Nice job, chaperone.

"Be ready in fifteen," she snaps by way of greeting. Starla gives her a thumbs up and a grin.

Inside the shower room, Gia sinks onto the bench with a sigh. Pulls out her comm, where Tevi's new contact card still blinks on the screen. She almost opens a message to him, but swipes it into her comm's archives instead; she's got more important matters to attend to than her rebellious libido.

She's not sure if communication within the station is monitored — fortunately, Calanthe Yang is a master of corporate espionage and information brokering, and on the weeks-long trip out to Durga's Belt, she had coached Gia through various scenarios they were likely to encounter and came up with a code for them to use just in case.

One that now makes Gia very uncomfortable.

She shakes the cobwebs from her mind and begins to type, cursing Calanthe's whimsy.

THINKING OF HOOKING UP WITH A GUY I MET YESTER-DAY. INCREDIBLY ATTRACTIVE, BUT SEEMS A BIT YOUNG. LOTS OF CONFIDENCE, THOUGH. WHAT DO YOU THINK? I CAN SEND PICS IF YOU HAVEN'T MET HIM.

Gia reads it through a couple of times to make sure the meaning is clear enough, then hits the shower, scrubbing her skin raw and scalding. She's getting dressed when the comm chimes again.

It's Calanthe:

I SAW HIM YESTERDAY, TOO, AND I SAY GET THAT SUGAR! YOUNG MAY BE RISKY, BUT A GIRL'S GOTTA LIVE! AND ANYWAY I'VE BEEN NOSING AROUND THE SCENE FOR US BOTH AND I BELIEVE HE'S THE MUCH SMARTER CHOICE. SEE YOU IN A FEW!

Gia takes a deep breath, parsing past the exclamation points to Calanthe's true meaning: Calanthe got the same offer Gia did, and the Yangs are putting their money on the union beating the cartel. Which means Jaantzen wants Gia to, too.

She scrolls through her past messages and finds one from Lorn that came in during the night. It looks like a junk invoice, the sort of thing designed to get the unwary to enter their account numbers so scammers can siphon out funds. But at a closer look, it's clearly from him. Gia fills out the form with the account numbers Jaantzen sent her, checks everything twice more before hitting send.

There's a sharp *tat-a-tat, tat-a-tat* on the door. Starla's knock.

"It's time," the girl signs.

I HEARD FROM JAANTZEN, Gia types, then shows the words on her screen to Starla. Her USL is way too bad to communicate this, and she won't risk saying it aloud. All this subterfuge has her paranoid, but it's certainly founded. She wouldn't be surprised if they're being bugged. *HE SAID THROW OUR WEIGHT BEHIND THE UNION. YANGS ARE TOO.*

Starla nods seriously, then takes Gia's comm to type her reply.

She hands the comm back.

HOW'S THE DOCTOR?

Starla winks.

"None of your goddamn business," Gia says. "Now let's go."

In Bulari the rich build their meeting spaces high in skyscrapers, perched like kings surveying their glittering city. But here on Maribi Station, the cartel buries deep. Intellectually, Gia knows this is safer — the deeper they go, the more protected from radiation they are. But in her gut she can feel the weight of the rock around them. It's like being buried alive.

Calanthe Yang meets them at the lift. Gia has met Calanthe's mother on more than one occasion, and she'd expected Calanthe to be as serious and austere as the old lady. But Julieta Yang's eldest daughter is ferociously energetic and unexpectedly bubbly, more like a successful businesswoman than the heiress to the empire of a smuggler extraordinaire.

Calanthe greets them both with exclamations of delight and air-kisses on the cheek that keep her dark purple lipstick firmly on her full lips. She's slim and poised, wearing an impeccable suit of dusty gray-blue wool so fine it shines and a soft peach silk blouse that matches the rose gold and mother-of-pearl combs in her glossy black hair.

Even during their weeks on the shuttle, Calanthe made Gia feel underdressed — and today is no exception. Starla's wearing something that says she belongs on the station, though Gia doesn't know enough about fashion to put her finger on how. Gia's wearing a simple, loose-fitting suit Manu picked out for her when she was worrying about what to wear before she left. It's one part comforting and one part heart-wrenching to be wearing something that reminds her of her best friend, still paralyzed from the waist down back home.

Not for the first time does she wish he was here in her place, as he should be. But since Gia isn't Manu the Silver-Tongued, she recognizes that she's here in part as muscle for

Calanthe, a reminder that the Yangs have powerful allies who win wars. Her job is to look tough and let Calanthe, the lawyer, do the talking.

"All good to go?" Calanthe says to Gia, and she's not just talking about whether or not she's ready for the meeting. Gia nods. "Us, too," Calanthe says. "Fantastic." She pushes the button to call the lift, and they don't say much after the doors close around them, just Calanthe exchanging the few pleasantries she's learned to sign with Starla.

When the doors open again, they're in the biggest room Gia has seen on the station. It's three times her height, and could easily fit a regulation boxing arena with seating for several hundred. It's done up in what she assumes is space station chic, all gold inlaid wire in geometric patterns across the walls, with black enamel accents and recessed lighting fixtures that wash sprays of light up onto the walls.

The room is big enough to host a sizable gathering, but right now their small group barely makes a dent in the space. Aiax Demosga, whose family owns a string of glitzy casinos in orbit around New Sarjun, is already sitting at the big round table. Beside him is a middle-aged man with smooth black skin wearing a suit of the type Gia associates with Indiran businessmen — something about the narrowness of the lapel, the flipped-up collar.

The name's Chevalier, she recalls from the briefing. If she remembers correctly, he deals mostly in weapons and has made most of his fortune supplying both sides of the civil wars on Indira.

Just because he sells guns doesn't mean he knows how to

use one, though, so she hasn't yet slotted him into the category of useful friend or viable threat.

Not that anyone has guns on the station. There's far too much potential of accidentally hitting something that could explode and destroy them all, or of puncturing an outer wall and sucking them all out into the vacuum of space through a hole the size of a fist. Or whatever terrifying shit happens out here in the black.

Some of the cartel soldiers carry stun carbines, and she's sure she seen at least one electric barb on a security guard's belt. But otherwise it's probably knife fighting if things happen to get out of hand. Not Gia's favorite, but she's not bad at it, either.

Aiax Demosga stands to greet her, his glittering smile, his loud shirt, even his sun-baked leather tan aggressive in this gray metal place. He shakes her hand; it's predictably finger-breaking.

"Giaconda, it's nice to meet you in person," he says. He shakes Starla's hand and trades air-kisses with Calanthe, then turns to his companion. "Calanthe, you've met Absolon Chevalier? Absolon, Giaconda Áte and Starla Dusai, Willem's representatives."

Chevalier's hand is slim and warm. "It's a pleasure," he says in a light Arquellian drawl. And to Starla, "I was very sorry to hear about your parents."

The slight wrinkle in Starla's brow tells Gia she's reading the transcription on her heads-up, and Chevalier notices the device at the same time. "My apologies," he says, and then signs something to her instead. Gia catches the signs for *parents, sorry*, but his hands are too fluid for her to follow with her limited USL.

He and Starla converse a moment longer before they all take their seats at the big circular table. It could fit another ten; like the enormous room, the table dwarfs their small group. It's almost as though it's by design, and it's starting to bother Gia.

"We're still missing a few," she says to Calanthe, who nods slowly, eyes narrowed as she scans the room.

"I didn't know you spoke USL," Demosga says, clapping Chevalier on the shoulder.

Chevalier shrugs. "Indira is a planet of many countries and many languages," he says simply. "I have endeavored to be fluent in all that I can."

Thankfully, before Chevalier can expound any more on how cosmopolitan and advanced Arquellians are, the door opens. Gia has done her homework, and although she doesn't recognize the knot of soldiers standing guard at the door, the head honcho of the Maribi Cartel is hard to miss.

Malcolm Saint would have stood out immediately for his swagger, even if she hadn't already recognized his face from her briefings: copper skin, round cheeks, a full head of thick hair, and a salt-and-pepper beard close-trimmed and neat. "I see we're all here," Saint says.

"We're waiting for a few more," Demosga answers.

A smile tugs at the corner of Saint's mouth, and unease churns in Gia's gut.

"It will just be us for the moment," Saint says. He sits at the far end of the table, a swath of seats between himself and his guests, then plants his elbows and interlaces his fingers, leaning forward so his chin rests on his knuckles. He gives them all a look in turn.

"I appreciate you all making the effort," he says. "And I've heard your complaints about our variable tariffs and service fees."

"Glad to hear it," Demosga says. He flashes his movie-star smile. "I've been going over the last decade's worth of records for our family's shipping expenditures, and I have some suggestions. Let's take a look at — "

"I wasn't quite finished," Saint says. His eyes glitter with malice. Gia can feel the mood go cold — this is not the posture of a man who's planning to negotiate. "The cartel will be standardizing the rates and service fees. Forty percent across the board."

Demosga lets out a shocked curse, but Calanthe just leans forward, smooth fingers steepled. "I think that's a bold opening position, Malcolm," she says.

"It's not a starting bid, Ms. Yang," Saint says. "It's our company's new standardized rate. You're welcome to find somewhere else to ship your goods."

Gia glances at Calanthe, who's wearing the slightly amused expression she and her mother both wield to devastating effect. "Believe me, my family is always looking for the best option. Unfortunately, the cartel has quite a monopoly out here."

"I would think you would be more interested in working with those who share your interests," says Chevalier calmly. "Without any legal recourse, it's best if we all work together."

"It wasn't a small journey to get here," Demosga snaps. "If

you had no intention of negotiating with us, why the hell invite us out here?"

"Oh, I had the intention of negotiating," Saint says slowly. He leans back in his chair, imperious. "I just thought I would be having this conversation with honorable business partners."

This time, Gia doesn't risk a glance at Calanthe. They've been found out. Which means Demosga and Chevalier were probably also approached by Lorn and his union of dockworkers. She feels a shift around the room, an atmospheric hush, clouds gathering before storm.

She catches Starla's eye. "Be ready," she signs.

Starla nods, shifting herself in her chair in a way that looks casual, though Gia can see alertness, readiness in the lines of her legs. There's no way she can let this come to a fight, though. They are outnumbered, members of the cartel stationed at the doors and fully armed.

"If you're not interested in negotiating, I have calls to make," Demosga says. He stands, and the cartel soldiers around the room reach for their weapons. Demosga looks around him with the steely-eyed glare of a man well seasoned by business negotiations in Bulari's underworld. "Unless of course, you're taking representatives from four of the biggest crime organizations on two planets hostage?" he asks.

"Sit down," Saint says. "We're not done talking." Demosga remains standing, his hands on the back of his chair.

Gia's running the odds. She doesn't have much hope in any of the others to have her back. Starla is scrappy but still new, and Calanthe and Demosga are much better known for their sharp business tongues than their knife skills, though Demosga has a reputation for bar brawls. And Chevalier?

There was nothing in the briefings she read about physical fighting.

Negotiation isn't her strong point, but they're all goners if this thing comes to violence.

"Have a seat, Demosga," she says. "The man just wants to talk."

Demosga turns his glare on her, then finally relents, settling back into his chair with his chin raised.

"We're all good," she says to Saint. "Let's chat."

Saint looks at her, and his lips move in what could be considered a smile, though there's nothing of warmth or camaraderie in it. "Who would've known the only person here with a cool head would be from Willem Jaantzen's crew?"

He clasps his hands together in front of him and leans forward like a teacher lecturing a group of disobedient schoolchildren. "You have all committed incredible trespass by speaking to somebody working against the cartel, let alone giving them money," he says. "If you were one of mine, you'd be dead. But, as Aiax pointed out, that would most likely lead to war with four of my best customers, who have powerful allies on both New Sarjun and Indira. So even though I would be completely justified — because it was you who first made aggressions against me — I will be the generous one."

Saint spreads his hands as though granting them a gift. "Tell me everything you know about this group, and I will happily continue doing business with you and with everyone else who has come here to negotiate today. At a flat forty percent rate to help remind you all that you do yourself no favors when you cross the Maribi Cartel." He smiles darkly.

"If any of your colleagues in the other families have a problem with that, I'll let them know to take it up with you directly."

"And you'll let us walk out of here," Demosga says.

"Of course. Provided your families see twice as much value in you as they were willing to give to my enemies."

"Ransom," says Chevalier.

Saint's smile is vicious. "Reparations." He shoves back his chair; it screeches on the polished floor. "I'll have you all escorted back to — "

Around the rooms, comms chime. Calanthe brushes a fingertip against her rose gold cuff; the corners of her lips tug down at the words displayed there. Starla's eyebrows arch as she reads the message on her heads-up. One of the cartel soldiers near the door swears loudly.

Saint's glare sweeps the room before he pulls his comm out.

Gia thumbs her own on.

CITIZENS, THIS IS A MESSAGE FROM THE UNITED DOCK-WORKERS OF MARIBI. BE ADVISED THAT ALL TRAFFIC AND SUPPLIES GOING IN OR OUT OF THE STATION WILL STOP UNTIL THE MARIBI CARTEL AGREES TO OUR TERMS. WE ARE A MOVEMENT OF MANY, SUPPORTED BY OTHER SECRETLY UNION-IZED WORKER GROUPS THROUGHOUT THE STATION. DO NOT TRY TO ENTER THE DOCKS. WE WILL SEND FURTHER COMMU-NICATIONS.

Beside her, Calanthe swears under her breath.

Whatever Lorn and his group were planning, it's beginning.

9

STARLA

The message from the union fades, and the screen of Starla's heads-up unit flickers. A yellow dot pulses in the upper left corner to tell her it's looking for signal, then goes solid green once more.

The strike has begun.

The room's energy has shifted abruptly from tensely crumbling negotiations to something even more uncertain. Calanthe is furiously conferring with Aiax; Gia's watching Saint, poised for action. Across the table, Absolon Chevalier catches Starla's eye and gives her a slight nod, but she's not certain what he's trying to convey.

A man comes in to whisper something in Saint's ear, and Saint sends two of his guards out the door with the messenger. Apparently whatever's going on out there is more threatening than the family representatives sitting at his conference table.

Saint turns back to the group with a smile.

"How fortunate," he says, his words scrolling across the

bottom of Starla's display. "I'm about to get a chance to demonstrate just why it was so unwise to bet against me."

He's a man who likes to talk, Starla thinks. She's used to being among people who choose their words carefully and without much fanfare. In her experience people who like to talk tend to overestimate their situations.

"Throwing your lot in with the dockworkers may have seemed like a good idea at the time," Saint says. "They told you we wouldn't see them coming, that they had the element of surprise. But believe me, they did not. I've known about their plans for months, and it's only been a matter of waiting for them to tip their hands." He smiles maliciously. "And, apparently, yours."

He glances at his comm as though judging the time. "Give us a few minutes and these traitors will be out an airlock."

Icy fear stabs through Starla's chest: Mona. She had been planning on escaping before all this went down, but there's no way she could have gotten off in time. Especially since she promised to at least say goodbye before leaving.

He's a man who likes to talk, Starla reminds herself. What he says has no bearing on what's actually happening.

"We have plenty of experience dealing with this sort of thing," Saint says. He stands. "Whatever little coup you all expected to happen is dead already. Let's put you somewhere for safekeeping. I'll — "

Starla feels the concussion in her chest, shivering through the station. The room goes dark, the pure, awful dark of Durga's Belt with not a scrap of sunlight to seep through the edge of a curtain or catch in a pane of glass. Here, the pressure of the black has physical weight, pressing like fingertips against Starla's eyes.

But only for a moment.

Emergency lights flicker on, transforming the gleaming gold threads in the wall into bloody, metallic streaks as the red light hits them.

"Get them out of here," someone says, the transcription crawling across her heads-up. Starla feels a hand on her arm, shrugs it off as she stands. In her pocket, her comm vibrates, and another message appears. From Mona.

WHERE ARE YOU, SHIT'S GOING DOWN.

Starla doesn't dare take her comm from her pocket to respond, not with all of these guards and guns surrounding her. And a moment later her chance is gone, anyway.

A second concussion, and the pulsing yellow light is back in her display. Only this time it flashes to red. They've done something to the network.

A guard grabs her arm, pulling her from her chair, and she shakes him off. Gia catches her arm before she can do anything, though, and motions in the dim light for Starla to follow her, with Calanthe in between them.

At the elevator, a guard is pressing the button without response. Once, twice, before he punches the wall beside the door. Starla can only assume the power has been cut to the elevators, too.

He turns to yell something at them, but without the network, Starla's heads-up isn't transcribing anymore. The useless thing is a mess of flashing red lights and error messages, so she unclips it and folds it into her pocket. She doesn't need the distraction.

Someone touches her shoulder and she glances back to see Aiax Demosga. He taps his temple, right where her heads-up had been. "Is everything all right?" she thinks he asks.

She pulls her comm from her pocket, taps it and shrugs. He frowns at her, then looks at his own comm. She sees the realization spread over his face as he notices the lack of connection. He says something else to her but she can't make it out — and then the guards are prodding them to another corner of the meeting room.

They're led to a cramped maintenance stairwell that looks like it doesn't get much use; Starla remembers similar stairs from Silk Station, lit only by dim strips of emergency lighting, the perfect place to get away for long heart-to-hearts with Mona where they wouldn't be underfoot — or found. These are cramped and narrow, almost as much climbing a spiral ladder as mounting stairs. They climb in single file, the stairs disappearing into gloom high above them; looking up she sees only the back of Calanthe's suit and Gia's legs beyond.

Aiax follows her, and the stranger with the dark skin and Indiran cut to his suit, Absolon Chevalier, takes up the rear. They climb for a few minutes before the group comes to a stop for no reason Starla can understand. She glances down, and Absolon catches her eye.

"Sounds like we stopped at a landing," he signs. His signs are slightly different from what she's become accustomed to on New Sarjun, but not so much so she can't understand him. He looks past her as though listening, then meets her gaze again. "We're going to climb on a few more floors. Can you fight?"

Starla nods, and Absolon gives her the ghost of a smile.

"Tell your friend," he signs. "Act when we get to the next landing."

They've started moving again, and Gia seems to be arguing with the guard above her, who Starla can't see. Starla grabs Calanthe's calf as they climb, and the woman looks down at her.

"Be ready," Starla signs, and seeing the V that forms between Calanthe's brows, she's not sure if the other woman understands. But Calanthe touches Gia's leg, and motions back down at Starla.

"Attack when you get just past the next landing," Starla signs, and she's one hundred percent sure Gia doesn't understand that. She sighs in irritation, mimes a gun, and points at the stairs. "2-0," she signs as she takes one step, then another. "1-9. 1-8. 1-7."

Gia gives her a nod and Starla takes a deep breath. The countdown has begun.

Hopefully.

She reaches the landing just as she feels the whole staircase shudder. She pulls Calanthe back down onto the narrow landing with her as Gia attacks the man above her and the Indiran begins to grapple with the guard below him. Starla tries the door handle, but although it's not locked, it's stiff with disuse. Aiax Demosga motions her out of the way, then uses his broad shoulder like a battering ram to burst through.

They spill out into another emergency-lit hallway. It's empty — for now — and Starla stands guard, the only thing she can do while Gia and Absolon finish off the guards inside the narrow staircase. The station shudders again, like a skipped heartbeat. Is this what Mona felt when Silk Station was being bombed apart by the Alliance? Starla had been on her parents' ship, the *Nanshe,* and there the attack had felt more immediate, more violent, flesh bruising against restraint belts as the ship lurched. Here the bombs feel more like a distant nightclub.

The fight is over as quickly as it began, and Absolon steps out of the stairwell, followed by Gia. She's got one of the guards' stun carbines slung over her shoulder. Absolon is bleeding from a gash on his temple and Gia has a split lip, but otherwise both seem fine.

"We need to get to safety," Gia says, and even without transcription, Starla has enough experience with Gia to feel confident in her lipreading.

Aiax Demosga, though? Not so much. He and Gia start arguing, and Calanthe cuts in. "We need to get to a ship," she says, as calm and easy to read as always.

"The docks are where all the fighting is happening," Gia says. "And we don't even know where we are."

Starla snaps her fingers for their attention. "I know," she signs. At least, she has a vague idea where they are, after all those hours spent studying the station maps trying to find Mona. And it doesn't hurt that she was born into the labyrinth of an asteroid station. She still has a map of the station down-loaded onto her comm, and though they won't be able to see where they are without the network, she should be able to figure that out. She opens the map and hands her comm over to Gia.

"We climbed nine flights," she signs, catching Absolon's eye in the hopes that he understands her.

Absolon nods. "Yes," he says clearly, signing slowly as he speaks. "I counted nine flights, too."

"But where are we," Gia asks. "That big-ass meeting room isn't anywhere on the map."

It wasn't, but Starla's been working out where it must be ever since they arrived in it. She scrolls through the station map in Gia's hand. Points to a spot. "We're here," she signs. "Here is the elevator shaft, and the stairwell doesn't seem to be marked."

"That seems right," Calanthe says after Absolon's finished interpreting. "Which means to get to the docks, we need to get to this stairway. Here."

Aiax grumbles something that looks like it could be about guards.

The stairway Calanthe is pointing at would deposit them in the passenger terminal outside the docks, but if the unionists are holed up in the docks like they said, the passenger terminal is probably teeming with cartel fighters trying to get in. That staircase is going to be suicide. Starla's not sure how to get into the docks, but she thinks she knows where Mona will be.

"We need to get into the docks, past the cartel," Starla signs. She points to the far end of the station map. "My cousin will probably be there, she'll get them to let us in. There's a secret stairway over here."

"A secret stairway?" Absolon says and signs. He doesn't seem to have much practice at it, and his USL is slower and clumsier than usual. "How do you know about it?"

"My cousin took me. It was being guarded by the dock-workers."

"Her cousin. It seemed like it was guarded by dockworkers," Absolon says to the others.

"Her cousin is who we need to get to," Gia says. "It doesn't matter if we get to a ship if they won't let us off the station."

Aiax seems to be objecting to the idea, but Calanthe holds up a hand. "After this, I doubt propriety matters to Saint," is what Starla thinks she says. "We are dead if we don't get off the station, and we certainly don't get off the station unless the dockworkers win. I may not be much of a fighter, but I know where to throw my lot."

Absolon nods. "The only sensible thing is to go find the leaders of this little rebellion and see what we can do to turn it in our favor," he says and signs. "Because we certainly know what will happen if the cartel wins."

"Unless anyone else has a secret private way off this rock," Gia says.

Finally, Aiax nods assent.

"Lead the way," Absolon signs to Starla.

It's smooth sailing for a few hundred meters, Gia and her stolen stun carbine taking lead while Starla points her in the right direction, Aiax and Absolon taking up the rear. Smooth sailing, that is, until a small knot of cartel soldiers catches sight of them when they round a corner about two-thirds of the way to the elevator.

Gia hits one in the chest right off the bat; he slumps to the ground, twitching. Another grabs for Starla, but Aiax is there beside her in a heartbeat. He pulls the cartel soldier off and knees him in the gut, then finishes him with a punch to the throat. It's not elegant, and it's certainly not what Gia has been teaching her. Aiax Demosga fights like a street brawler, and the way he cracks his knuckles and goes after the other guy, it looks like he enjoys cracking heads.

Gia takes out the third soldier, then turns to watch Aiax headbutt the last one. Although it doesn't look necessary to Starla, he does it again for good measure. Calanthe is watching him with a raised eyebrow.

"Come on, Aiax," says Calanthe. "You enjoyed that far too much."

Aiax opens his mouth to answer, but there's a flash of movement down the hall behind him, and before anyone can react a fifth cartel soldier steps from a doorway and flings a knife into Aiax's back.

And then the soldier goes down in a limp tangle of limbs, the result of a brilliant flash from some small device Absolon Chevalier is holding in the palm of his hand. Stella catches only a glimpse of it before he flips it back into his pocket: it's shiny, all chrome and inlaid lapis lazuli. She would mistake it for a cigarette case if she saw it lying on a table.

Whatever it did, her skin is crawling from the residual effects. Beside her, Calanthe runs her hands over her forearms with a suppressed shudder.

Absolon is a weapons dealer, Starla reminds herself — and apparently he has access to some pretty interesting stuff. She'll have to ask him about it later, because right now, Aiax Demosga is slumped on the floor, breath coming shallow and lips forming unintelligible shapes that might or might not be words.

"We're not far from that clinic your friend works at," Starla signs to Gia. "We have to get him there."

Gia frowns at her. "We're not where?"

"Apparently there is a medical center nearby," Absolon says to her. He turns to Starla. "On this level?" he signs.

She shakes her head. Points up at the ceiling and holds up two fingers for Gia's benefit.

She sees realization dawn on Gia's face. "The clinic," Gia says. "We can't all go. Demosga, can you walk?" She slips her arm underneath and helps him to his feet. His knees buckle once, then he braces himself and nods.

"Stay with them," he says — Starla thinks he says.

"No one else is strong enough to help you," Gia says. She helps him lean against the wall, then turns to Starla. "You'll be all right," she signs to Starla, and whether it's a command or a reassurance, Starla can't tell from Gia's usual fierce expression. "Get them to Mona and safety. I'll get Demosga to help."

Starla fights back a thrill of fear and adrenaline. Gia will be fine. She'll be fine. Mona will be fine — so long as she steps it up and acts right now. Absolon and Calanthe both look to her for guidance, and she tamps down any fear she might feel.

"Stay behind me," she signs, pointing to Calanthe. She turns to Absolon. "And you, take up the rear." Absolon nods his assent, and they head off down the hallway.

As they pass the cartel soldier Absolon took out, Starla can't help but stare. He's not bonelessly slumped like the men Gia shot with the stun carbine. This one's all frozen limbs and sharp angles, like a dead spider curled in on itself. Calanthe's eyes widen. But when Starla meets Absolon's gaze, he only smiles.

10

GIA

Demosga is heavy, but one benefit of the lighter gravity on Maribi Station is that he's not as much of a burden as he would be back on New Sarjun. Even so, by the second flight up he's stumbling more than ever, and he slips from her grasp entirely in the stairwell. Gia curses. If any enemy comes across them now, they're both dead.

The network seems to still be out station-wide, and beyond emergency lighting, all of the electrical system seems to be down, too. Except for the intercom, and a pleasant male voice has been talking to them on repeat, telling everyone to return to their quarters or risk detainment, as they'll be assumed to be a member of the striking forces.

The people they do see seem to either be obeying the command or actively seeking to join in the fight, though Gia can't tell for which side.

And she's not the only one helping someone with an injury.

The scene at the clinic is just as chaotic as Gia had antici-
pated. The waiting room is even more filled with people than
it was yesterday, but fewer of them are patients. Instead it's
become a staging area of equipment and supplies, medics in
uniform rushing to get everything prepared.

Tevi Sharaf is directing traffic in the middle of the room,
wearing the formal white Sulila jacket that means he's
prepared to assert his status if need be. "We'll need another
set of those," he says to a nurse. "And the mobile burn unit —
get it ready and meet us there. We need to — Gia?"

Other faces turn to them, and a nurse — a man closer to
Demosga's size — hurries over to help her. Gia straightens in
relief as the big man's weight lifts off her shoulders. Demosga's
been losing a steady stream of blood and is starting to lose
consciousness, too.

That burden's gone, but Gia steels herself for her next
task: ignoring the wide-eyed look Tevi is giving her and telling
herself he's just another guy in scrubs at just another triage
scene that she needs to deal with.

"He got stabbed in the back," she says to the nurse. "The
knife's still there, but he's losing blood fast." The sleeve of her
suit jacket is heavy with blood, but it's not hers; she ignores it.
The nurse helps Demosga onto a gurney — it was probably
waiting to be wheeled down to the scene of the fighting — and
Demosga's eyes flutter open.

He blinks at her, gaze focusing on her face. Beneath his
coppery tan, his face is bloodless.

"Sir? Sir, we're going to get you into surgery right away,"
the nurse says.

Demosga winces as the nurse begins to wheel the gurney

away, then reaches to catch Gia's hand. The nurse stops, glancing between them.

"I owe you for this one," Demosga says, his normally booming voice quiet.

"I'll let the man know," Gia says. She doesn't know what kind of tally sheet Demosga and her boss have, but right now doesn't seem like a good time to start caring. She's got bigger things to worry about. "Now let these guys take care of you."

"Not Jaantzen," Demosga says. "I meant you."

"Just don't die," Gia says, extricating her hand. She's not sure what favors one can ask from a man like Aiax Demosga, but she hopes she's never in a position to need one.

She watches as he's wheeled through the doorway, then turns back to Tevi, who — she realizes too late — has been standing silent behind her through this entire exchange. The look he's giving her could make the deserts of New Sarjun feel arctic.

He heard the name. And of course he will recognize it.

"Tevi — "

"I don't disagree that you can save a lot more lives with a gun then a med kit sometimes," he says quietly. "But I know the names of some of those who have put bodies in my emergency room. Especially lately."

"Tevi."

"Who you work for now, that's your choice," he says bitterly. "Just tell me the rest of it wasn't true, all those things they said about you when you were on trial." The look in his eyes is both pleading and despairing, like he wants desperately to believe what she's about to tell him, but is afraid he can't.

"It wasn't true," Gia says quietly.

"But now — " He doesn't seem quite ready to say it. "You work for Willem Jaantzen."

"I'm making the right choice." She can't explain it, what sets this one man apart from the woman who sent her to prison. And she shouldn't need to explain it. She made the decisions she needed to when she left Redrock, and Tevi has made decisions of his own. There's no reason either of them should have to explain anything to each other.

Gia looks around the room, at the med kits and people in disarray. They're all trying to pretend they're not watching the scene in front of them.

"It looks like you're going into a war," she says finally. "Do you need someone who knows how to hold both a scalpel and a gun, or not?"

11

STARLA

Despite her map, the station is like a maze, and more than once Starla leads Calanthe and Absolon into a dead end before figuring out the right turn and finally arriving at the room Mona had led her to last night. The forklift suit is still leaning in the hallway, slumped in on itself in an eerie mimicry of the cartel solder Absolon zapped.

Starla tries the handle. Locked. She knocks, the same *tat-a-tat, tat-a-tat* she used to use to get Mona's attention when she was supposed to be studying in her room, but nothing happens. She frowns at Absolon, jerking her chin at the door.

"I don't hear anyone inside," he says.

Starla tries the handle again, then Calanthe Yang taps her on the shoulder and produces a tab the size of her thumbnail, which she affixes to the lock. It begins to glow a pearly, opalescent orange. Calanthe types a code into her comm, and the device blinks three times, then shifts to a cheerful green.

The handle turns under Starla's palm.

Calanthe just smiles and uses one lacquered thumbnail to peel the device back off, pocketing it. "A very useful bit of tech," she says clearly, so Starla can lipread. "I'll show you how to use it on the flight back home."

If they get a flight back home, Starla thinks, then dashes the thought away. They certainly won't if she starts down that path.

Starla pushes through the door with a rush of anticipation and dread as to what she'll find inside.

And — nothing.

The monitors, the terminals, the swags of wires — everything but the tables has been cleared out. Starla groans in frustration. She could lead them to Mona's room, but if she's pulled up roots here, what's to make Starla think she'll be there?

"What is this place?" Calanthe asks.

"Used to be my cousin's lab," Starla signs.

"Your cousin's lab," repeats Absolon, signing and speaking. "Where is she now?"

Starla shrugs, exasperated and embarrassed at having brought these two — business partners of her godfather's — to a dead end. She turns in frustration to scan the room. If nothing else, at least they'll be safe here for the time being. Then maybe she can head out on her own to try to find Mona.

"We'll be safe here until we can contact her, or another member of the union," she signs.

"If it's safe, we should stay here for now," Calanthe says, and Starla's not sure if she understood her signs and is agreeing with her, or if she's making her own suggestion.

"I'm not interested in sitting around," Absolon says and

signs gamely. "We should find the head of the union and offer our help."

"But how do we find them without running into the cartel?" Starla asks.

Before Absolon can answer, a flash of movement at the door behind him catches Starla's eye. Absolon spins with his palm outstretched, the same silvery cigarette-box-shaped weapon in his hand.

Starla shouts at him before he fires, grabbing his arm.

Ahmed stands in the doorway, clutching a black duffel to his chest like a shield.

He looks wide-eyed between Calanthe and Absolon before settling on Starla.

"What are you doing here?" he asks.

Starla nudges Absolon. "This is a friend of my cousin. Explain to him that we need to find her."

Absolon's explanation is longer than Starla thinks it needs to be, but judging by Calanthe's expression it doesn't seem to be going off base.

When Absolon finishes speaking, Ahmed nods. "I can get you to see her, but there's one problem. She's in the docking bay. It's the heart of all the fighting."

"That's where we need to be, too," Starla signs.

Ahmed nods. "Let's go."

Ahmed leads them to a back passageway. No one seems to be guarding the entrance, but when they slip through the hatch they get a face full of plasma carbine barrel. To Starla, the thought of what might happen if someone fired one of those things on a space station is almost as gut-clenching as the thought of being its target.

But the guard lowers his weapon when he sees Ahmed.

Starla's heart rate drops back to normal. For a second, at least, until a man stalks over to them and begins yelling unintelligibly.

Starla may have navigated them here; now it's Calanthe Yang's turn to be in her element. She steps forward, all polished lawyer. Starla can only catch snatches of what Calanthe is saying, and she can't read the burly man's lips at all, but the way the conversation goes is evident by their body language. The station-born man towers above Calanthe, and he uses his height to intimidate, standing a little too close and bowed forward, forcing Calanthe to arch her back to see him. If it makes her uncomfortable, though, she's far too poised to let it show.

He's fighting a battle of aggression; Calanthe is all about the smooth, calm persuasion. Her expression, her mannerisms, everything is polite yet strong, and when she refuses to budge, he finally acquiesces, takes a step back. She straightens, chin lifted and smile professional.

This entire trip, Starla has thought that Calanthe was the weak link when compared to Gia. Now she revises her estimation of the woman. Where Gia uses her muscles and weapons skills, Calanthe does battle in a way that can be just as effective. Maybe Starla has something to learn from her after all.

Calanthe motions Starla forward. "We're looking for her cousin," she says.

Ahmed says something that Starla doesn't catch, and the man finally looks at Starla, assessing her.

"She told me about you," he says finally — at least, she thinks he says. "Come with me."

Starla hasn't been back to the docking bay since the day they arrived — access is restricted to dockworkers and passengers who are actively embarking or disembarking. It's three times as wide as the busy passenger terminal on the other side of the long wall, with smaller ships clamped into neat rows and materials handling equipment parked around them. She doesn't see the shuttle they came in on; presumably it's already left, packed with people on their way back to the inner planets.

People who got off this rock just in the nick of time.

Instead of the hustle and bustle Starla remembers from their first day here, there's now a different sort of energy. One area, near the center, seems to be set up as a support station, with people putting out food and handing out weapons. The four sets of bay doors that lead to the passenger terminal are shut tight, but it doesn't look like the dockworkers think that will keep the cartel out for long. They're parking machinery in a barricade, arranging stacks of cargo crates to use for cover if it comes to a fight.

Mona had told her that they'd been hiring mercenaries, but their supply of weapons still looks meager, especially compared to what little Starla has seen of the cartel. A small squadron of men and women are running through drills in an open space at the far end of the docks. It looks like they've drilled before, but none of them move like they've fought together.

Starla's heart sinks. The union is going to need much more than a few extra fighters if they're not all going to be crushed into dust.

Starla scans the crush of people before remembering that the Mona she was getting used to yesterday has already shifted like a chameleon. Right — she's looking for a short black bob, not the magenta mane.

She spots her about fifty meters away, hunched over a makeshift web of monitors and terminals, her newly black curls wrenched into a tangled knot on top of her head. Relief washes over Starla. She heads that way with Calanthe and Ahmed at her side, only to realize she's lost track of Absolon. She knows no one else here is her responsibility, but she feels a sense of obligation to her godfather's name to make sure they all get through this all right.

She spins, scanning the room, and spots the dark Indiran man examining the barricade of machinery the dockworkers have put up.

He glances over as she walks up. "I saw one of these over by the room where we met your friend," he signs. "Do you know what it is?"

"It's a forklift suit," Starla signs. It's a newer-looking model than the ones she's familiar with, and it looks much more comfortable and maneuverable then the ones she remembers in her parents' docking bay. It even has a chestplate and clear safety shield over the face to protect the user against crushing injuries.

"The dockworkers might outnumber the cartel, but they're certainly outgunned," Absolon signs. "Unfortunately, my entire inventory is ship and station weapons systems — far too powerful to use inside the station, even if a human could lift the artillery."

"An unaided human," Starla signs, and Absolon nods thoughtfully, tilting his head to consider the suit.

Starla runs her hands over the forklift suit, examining the attachment system and auxiliary clamps. They look proprietary, designed to be used only with branded add-ons, but the dockworkers could always weld something directly to the arm. And one of the suits has a dexterous-looking drum-handling clamp that just might be useful.

"Show me what you have. We could modify weapons to mount on these suits."

"But the firing interface?" Absolon signs. "Ah. You said your cousin is a hacker." He smiles. "Then let's go find her. And see if someone will let me onto my ship."

12

GIA

Someone gave her a medical tunic emblazoned with the clinic's logo to replace her bloody suit jacket, and the surgical cap she found in a closet should be making her look a lot less like an escaped prisoner you should shoot at and more like a doctor you shouldn't. She lays her stolen stun carbine on top of other supplies in a duffel bag and leaves the seam unsealed when she shoulders it so she can grab the gun quick if she needs to.

Tevi doesn't say a word to her, doesn't look her way. But he doesn't send her away, either, and Gia joins the rest in the trek to the passenger terminal.

Last time she was here it was all souvenir shops and tourist-trap restaurants. Now the storefronts are all shut tight and the wide promenade in front of them is teeming with cartel soldiers. The bay doors along the longest wall, that lead to the docking bay, are all shut tight, and by the frustrated way one soldier is mashing at a control panel, the union has them locked out.

Tevi pauses briefly and scans the scene; when his eyes meet hers it seems like an accident, and he looks quickly ahead. "Everyone stay back," he says. "I'm going to go find out who's in charge."

"Everyone" clearly means her, too, but Gia ignores him. She walks a few paces behind, duffel bag open and over her shoulder, trying her best to look like a nurse in generic scrubs and not like she's going to kill anyone who puts a hand on him.

There'd been fighting here before those doors closed, and recently. A few bodies are slumped along the wall, but there are also injured people — cartel members and dockworker prisoners — who need immediate attention.

Gia ducks her head. Few of the cartel members should know her by sight, and if she's lucky they'll simply ignore her. She's seen it happen often enough in the past, her uniform blending in with the chaos of the scene, no one taking time to stop and look at a face.

A rangy man with tattoos scrawled up his cheeks stops Tevi with a scarred hand on his chest. "What the hell you want?" he asks.

"I'm here to speak with whoever's in charge," Tevi says. "We're here to help anyone who needs it."

The rangy man curls his lip. "No one is injured, and even if they were, these people don't need your help."

Tevi looks pointedly to the right, where a man in a dock-worker's uniform is shackled and huddled against the wall, cradling a broken arm, blood streaming from a cut on his forehead.

"He looks like he needs help," Tevi says.

"He's going out an airlock," the soldier says.

"Absolutely not. The Sulila charter states that in wartime — "

"Who says we're at war?"

It's a new voice joining the conversation, coming low and lethal over Gia's left shoulder. She turns towards it, right hand dropping into the open duffel at her side, but the man the voice belongs to — a cartel lieutenant whose picture Gia remembers seeing in a dossier — walks past her to confront Tevi.

Tevi stands his ground, every bit as cool under the murderous attention of well-armed cartel soldiers as he ever has been in an emergency room. If Gia hadn't already screwed this one up, she'd let herself be proud.

The lieutenant — Baxir, his name finally comes to her in a flash — glares at Tevi. "Who says we're at war?" he asks again.

"I misspoke," Tevi says calmly. "There are hostilities between two parties, and I brought my team to tend to the injured." He motions to the shackled dockworker with the broken arm, then turns to a cartel member who's still got a gun in his hand, even with the bloody knife slash across his thigh. "You have to let us help these people."

Baxir gives him an impatient look. "I don't have to do anything. Your little clinic is here because we let you be here, but the cartel says what goes. You're welcome to help Maribi citizens, but none of the prisoners."

Tevi shakes his head. "Sulila code is to treat all, no matter their background or status."

"Cartel code is to fuck those who try to fuck us," Baxir

snarls. "Don't get on that list." He turns to acknowledge a woman who's appeared at the edge of the group. "Are you ready?" he asks.

"Yessir," she says. "The dock is fully sealed for breach."

"Where is Saint?"

"On his way."

"Good. He'll give the order."

Gia's mouth goes dry, and she turns to look at the bay doors. If Starla and Calanthe made it, they'd be just on the other side of that wall, no way to get out. She'd misunderstood what the cartel soldier was doing to the door panel when they first came in. He wasn't trying to get in — he was making sure the people inside couldn't get out.

"There are innocent people in there," Tevi says. "You can't just open the airlocks."

"If they were innocent, they wouldn't be in there," Baxir says. "Although, come to think of it, your team is welcome to go into the docking bay and tend to anyone injured inside. Be our guests."

"Murdering Sulila staff is a war crime," Tevi says, venom in his voice.

"Then it's a good thing we're not at war," Baxir says with a grin.

"Tevi," Gia says softly. They need to get a message to Starla, and standing around arguing with this asshole isn't going to get them anywhere. He doesn't hear her or he's still ignoring her, and she reaches to touch his arm.

Someone grabs Gia's shoulder, wrenching her back around.

"Hey!" shouts Tevi. "Leave my people alone."

Gia drops the duffel as she pulls the stun carbine free. She's too close range to use it on the man who grabbed her, but she slams the stock into his knuckles to break his grip and punches the butt into his sternum.

It thuds against his armor, and before she can strike again the man pushes her back with a roar. She stumbles. Meaty hands close around her upper arms before Gia can catch her footing; a torso like a wall of muscle is at her back.

Malcolm Saint steps towards her, rubbing the knuckles she split with the stun carbine. He wrenches it from her hands, all bared teeth and ferocious grin.

"She isn't one of yours," he says to Tevi. He turns back to Gia. "Where are the rest of the traitors?"

"None of your goddamn business," Gia spits. She's not afraid for herself; that ice-cold stab of guilt is for what she may have brought on Tevi and his team. Her biceps ache where the goon behind her is squeezing, thick fingers digging into muscle.

She can't see him, but his bulk feels impressive, and even if she could take him and Saint and Baxir down, this whole passenger terminal is packed with well-armed cartel members.

And even if she were willing to go out in her own blaze of glory, she couldn't risk what would happen to Tevi and the others if she tried.

"Let me go," Gia snarls. "Or forget doing business with anyone back on New Sarjun."

Saint grabs her throat, face close to hers. His breath is hot, sharp; somewhere outside her field of immediate attention, she hears Tevi yelling.

"What risk?" Saint asks. "Doing business with some thugs

from Bulari? Losing a couple of your boss's friends as my customers? Sweetheart, I don't give a shit what your boss thinks of me."

13

STARLA

Absolon's ship is parked at the far end of the docking bay.

It's nothing much to look at from the outside, all unpainted metal plating and unbuffed rivets. But the complicated set of biolocks Absolon has to activate to gain access says there's something interesting inside.

It reminds Starla of her parents' ship. Starla grew up on the *Nanshe* — at least, when it was in dock. Then, she'd spend long hours feeding wires with skinny fingers through narrow spaces for her mother or holding metal sheeting in place for her father while he patched up the holes that got punched through their bow with startling regularity. She hadn't been allowed to go with them on any of their raids.

Except for the last one, which was the only reason she'd ended up in Alliance custody rather than blown to shrapnel or scattered to the wind like the rest of the inhabitants of Silk Station.

At the thought, she glances involuntarily over her shoulder to where Mona is hunched about twenty paces away, staring at her hand terminal, which is plugged into a port in the forklift suit. She's frowning at whatever she sees, but looks up as though sensing Starla's attention.

"Is everything good?" Mona signs, a little flick of her gaze indicating Absolon.

"Don't worry about him," Starla signs back. He may be Arquellian, but Absolon definitely isn't tied to the Alliance. She knows that's not the only qualification for being trustworthy, but he seems all right to her.

Absolon types in a complicated code and a ladder descends from the belly of the ship. "Welcome, welcome," he signs, beckoning for Starla to follow him up the ladder; he's pretending not to have noticed the exchange between her and Mona.

The ladder leads directly into the cramped cabin, where there's barely room for the two of them to stand. Starla wonders if Absolon runs with a crew, or if it's just him piloting alone through the vacuum for weeks on end. Although, if this ship is anything like the *Nanshe*, it took him a lot less time to get here — even from Indira — than it took Starla and Gia to get here on the slow shuttle from New Sarjun.

Absolon's scanning the cabin as if out of habit, as if looking for anything out of place rather than looking for something specific. A little nod of satisfaction to himself and he motions for Starla to go through the small hatch behind her.

Much like the *Nanshe*, Absolon's ship is designed with a preference towards zero-G navigation. The passageway Starla's clambering through would be a simple shaft to float down when weightless, but in dock it's a cramped corridor, and Starla ducks low to navigate it. Fortunately, it's not very long.

Though Absolon's ship looks reasonably roomy from the outside, inside it's compactly designed. A pair of open bunks are built into the corridor walls; beyond them, a series of roll-up panels are labeled things like Rehydrator and Sanitizer and Waste. The labels are all situated to be read right-way-up if you're floating up the shaft with your head aimed at the cabin — instead of a real kitchenette and crew quarters like the *Nanshe* had, you're meant to float in the corridor while taking care of your food input and waste output needs.

It's not the most comfortable setup Starla has ever seen, but it's impressively utilitarian.

And once Starla reaches the end of the corridor, she sees just why the designers cut down on space for the humans operating the ship. The corridor opens into a room five times Starla's height wide and ten times as long. At least two-thirds of the ship is dedicated to cargo space.

She climbs down the ladder to what is currently the floor, though there are crates strapped to scaffolding on all the surfaces around her. Elastic webbing suspends a cube of shelving units packed with crates in the middle of the room, and there's just enough space for her and Absolon to stand on the operations platform at the bottom of the ladder. If she cranes her neck, she can see cargo packed in crawlspaces back around the central corridor, too.

When he joins her, Absolon calls up a screen and begins scanning through what looks like a manifest. Light streams around his dark fingers as he finds what he's looking for. "This is it," he signs, pinching open a line item that reads: T53No1 Flamethrower LX-4 Med

He types in a command and Starla feels the shiver around her of the ship coming to life, looks around the room until she sees the robotic arm swiveling on a gimbal to pick a crate and deposit it near the stern of the ship.

Absolon's scanning through the manifest again. Starla stops him. "This. What is it?"

Absolon shakes his head. "Those cannons would tear a hole through the side of the station."

"Right." Starla points at another item in the manifest. "But what if we modified it to shoot this, instead?"

A slow grin spreads over Absolon's face. "That might just work." His finger reaches to touch the line item, but they stop just short, flexing as though he's contemplating saying something else to her. He takes a deep breath, then he activates the picking arm and turns to her with a sad smile.

"I knew your parents," he signs. "In fact I worked with them a time or two, before you were born. Maybe I'll tell you some stories once we're through the other side of this." He stops, considering his next words. Starla is still; one breath will ruin the moment.

"If I know anything about them, they'd be proud of you," Absolon signs, and the moment is past, anyway. As it should be, considering the circumstances; a bitterness rises in the back of her throat.

"We should get these crates to the rest," signs Absolon. He steps off the platform, drops to the catwalk graceful as a dancer.

Starla's heart is racing, but she climbs down after him,

batting the sudden flurry of questions she wants to ask out of her mind.

Now isn't the time.

Absolon palms the cargo ramp, and the one part of the ship designed to be more functional while docked than not descends into Maribi Station's docking bay. He's already slaved a pair of pallet jacks to his comm, and they scurry up the ramp to retrieve his cargo, then zip with the crates down the ramp and over to where Mona, Ahmed, and a crew of dockworkers have assembled a squadron, a yellow-and-black army of forklift suits.

The suits are slumped in rest, like an army already defeated.

Or one about to rise.

A woman's yelling at Starla as she pries open the crate of flamethrowers, jaw wide and hands gesticulating in nonsense. Starla frowns, then recognizes her: the woman driving the forklift suit who had been shouting at her shortly before she found Mona, or Mona found her. Was that only yesterday?

"I'm deaf," Starla signs, and the woman mouths something back. Starla points to both ears, shakes her head, does the flat-hand *null* handsign, and after a confused blink, the woman points at her own ears and yells something. Starla shakes her head with an expression like *I'm afraid not*, assuming they're having a conversation.

The woman nods slowly, then points at the flamethrower, then the forklift suit. She wraps gloved hands around the far end of one of the heavy weapons and pretends to heft it, then lifts her eyebrows. That, at least, is clear: *Can I help carry?*

It's short work, and the attachment clamps aren't as difficult to modify as Starla expected. The yelling woman catches on quick, grabbing another pair of forklift operators and explaining the process to them so that the work can go twice as fast. Mona's hack to the firing systems is easily replicated from machine to machine, and soon a half-dozen forklift suits are outfitted and ready to go. The yelling woman climbs into the first one and straps herself into the controls, grinning. Beyond her, another team have mounted the modified cannons to pallet jacks and are running them through maneuvers.

Starla's about to sign for the yelling woman to test the flamethrower when she feels a hand on her upper arm, the friendly squeeze and trailing downward brush that can only be Calanthe. Starla turns with a triumphant smile. Calanthe's face says, *We have a problem.*

She hands Starla a comm; a feed is already running. "We need to get out there," Calanthe says; it's directed to someone just beyond Starla.

Starla turns to see the burly station-born commander of the dockworkers. He's scowling at the forklift suits with something that might be approval, but he shakes his head at Calanthe's request, barks some kind of command.

Mona slips up beside Starla, bicep warm against hers. "He says we need more time," Mona signs, then cranes her neck to look at the comm Calanthe handed Starla. Starla feels her stiffen, then looks herself.

It's blurry, but Starla would know that bullheaded surgeon anywhere.

Gia is in the center of the passenger terminal. She's wearing a medic's jacket, standing near her doctor friend in his white Sulila uniform. A half-dozen others in the same white uniform are huddled a bit farther back — and for good reason. Gia and her doctor are surrounded by a squadron of cartel soldiers, and it doesn't look like things are going well.

Starla squints at the screen.

Is that Saint?

She's shouting in her head at the screen but Gia can't hear. Almost too late, Gia grabs a stun carbine from the duffel over her shoulder and whips around to face Saint — but she's too close to use the weapon and he pushes her back into a mountain of a man, whose hands close around her arms like steel clamps.

Starla shoves the comm back at Calanthe. "We don't have any more time," she signs to Mona. She waves an arm at the forklift operator woman, points her towards the door. The woman grins and the ground shakes as she and the other operators take their first thudding steps towards the door.

And the shaking stops.

Starla turns back, confused.

The commander's waving his arms to stop the forklift operators. He rounds on Starla, clearly unhappy that she's taken control of his — dammit, *her* — fleet of forklift suits.

"What's your problem?" Starla signs, exasperated. "We have to get out there."

"We have enough to do without saving some Sulila doctors," the commander says; Mona's slipped into Starla's line of sight, interpreting. "If they want to get themselves into this mess, they can get themselves back out."

"They're not just doctors, they're my friends," Starla signs. "Though that shouldn't matter one goddamn bit." She sweeps an arm over her tiny army. "Because how many of you have been fixed up at that clinic?"

The commander turns to glare at Mona as she says it, but some of the forklift operators straighten.

"That's what I thought," Starla continues, and whatever the commander snarls at her, she ignores it before Mona has a chance to interpret. She's not looking at him anymore, anyway. "Are your weapons working?" she signs, and a half second after Mona repeats it there's an answering chorus of flame and heat.

Starla shares a grin with the yelling woman, then sprints to the nearest bay door. It's closed — she lifts her hands to it, gives the man at the control panel a *What the fuck* look.

"I couldn't get it open if I wanted to," the man answers — Mona's sprinted ahead with Starla to interpret, though her dusky face is ashen with fear. "They've locked it from the outside."

"They've sealed it?"

Mona nods in affirmation, and Starla's mouth goes dry. "They're not going to — "

Just then, the lights in the docking bay dim once, twice, three times. Everyone around Starla stills and turns their gazes to the ceiling, listening to whatever alarm is sounding.

Mona's wide eyes meet hers, but Starla doesn't have to ask to know what the alarm means.

Those doors aren't just locked, they're sealed.

For vacuum.

Starla grabs Mona's arm and runs to the control panel — her cousin's the hacker, but maybe her knowledge of mechanics and engineering will help. She's so focused on the red blinking screen beside the bay door that she doesn't even notice Absolon standing next to it, not until a flash of silver in her peripheral vision catches her attention.

He's holding a weapon she's never seen before, but if she had to guess it's a mix between a plasma carbine and a laser, with a splash of concussion shot thrown in for good measure.

He proffers it with a small smile — it's far lighter than she expected, but of course that's the gravity here. The chrome feels like silk in her palms.

Absolon points at the center of the door.

"I'll need that back when you're done," he signs.

Starla grins.

She fires.

14

GIA

"Let her go," Tevi is saying, and it's that same calm, well-reasoned voice he uses on patients who come in way too high on some street drug. Or on mothers who are clinging catatonically to the bodies of their children. "She's a Sulila doctor. She's with my team."

"She try to pull one over on you, too?" Saint says to him. He tugs the surgical cap off Gia's head, turns her chin to look at the tattoos behind her ears. "This one's nothing but a double-crossing criminal." His grip tightens around Gia's throat; her lungs buck in her chest, burning for breath.

"Please take your hands off my doctor," Tevi says, voice an edge of steel.

Saint smiles at Gia, eyes glittering points as the margins of her vision darken. "Okay," he says.

His grip loosens and she gasps for air. Then he spins, punches Tevi in the gut, driving his knee into Tevi's chin when he doubles over. Tevi drops to his hands and knees.

Gia doesn't realize she's screamed until Saint looks back at her, the corner of his mouth quirking up. She's made the oldest mistake in the book — she's let him know that Tevi is a way to hurt her.

Saint kicks Tevi once in the ribs then hauls back for another. And Gia shoots out a quick, frantic prayer to the gods of reduced gravity that the muscle behind her doesn't drop her. She drives her knees up to her chest and kicks out as hard as she can, putting the full force of her boots into Saint's hip. The goon behind her grunts and staggers back, but his iron claws in her biceps continue to hold her weight. They pierce like spikes.

Saint's already off-balance, about to kick; he crashes to one knee, but then he's up on his feet again with a speed driven by fury. He turns on her with a hiss of pain, a limping step to close the distance between them.

If she lets him see old age, that joint's gonna give him troubles.

"I'm done with you," he snarls, grabbing her throat once more. His free hand pats at her hips, then worms into the front pocket of Gia's slacks, slipping back out with her comm. He lets go of her throat, then forces her thumb onto the pad to unlock it.

"Contacts, contacts. There we are," he says. "Recording a message for Willem Jaantzen."

He clears his throat. "Jaantzen, you piece of shit," he says. "You think you can send your people to my house and throw me out my own airlock? You think the Maribi Cartel is a bunch of weak-ass punks just waiting to roll over for you? I've got your woman, and I'll find your little girl. And you send anyone else close to Durga's Belt, they'll get a bullet in the head, too."

He turns the comm back to face Gia, then pulls his pistol from his waistband and shoves the barrel under her chin. The small part of her that's still paying attention to the world outside of Saint and that gun notices the muscle behind her flinch and try to distance himself. The iron grip loosens just a fraction.

Out of the corner of her eye she can see the recording image: her dark face shining with sweat, brown eyes wide. She forces her attention away, doesn't let it distract her.

"Any last words for your boss?" Saint asks with a mocking grin.

"No!"

Saint's attention wavers for a split second as Tevi rushes him, and Gia shoves her weight to one side, slamming a forearm into Saint's to push the gun in the opposite direction. She feels the concussion in her eardrum like a sharp silver spike, and all sound is replaced by a high, tinny whine.

The grip on her biceps goes slack and the muscle behind her slumps to the ground.

Tevi has Saint locked in an awkward hug, but Saint is quickly getting the upper hand. Baxir rushes in to pull Tevi off, and Gia elbows him in the throat, kicks him in the groin, and he goes down. Another bullet whizzes by Gia to bury itself in the wall. Saint, his aim going wild as Tevi wrestles for control. Another shot, and Tevi yowls in pain and falls to the floor, blood blooming from his thigh.

Gia tackles Saint from behind as he levels his gun at Tevi's head, sending the weapon skittering across the floor.

She punches him once at the base of his skull and he flips her — he's stronger, even if his technique is sloppy and his hip is injured. She breaks his grasp and notices his fingers straining towards his boot. There — a flash of a knife. With all of her strength, Gia throws him off-balance and back into a crate, spine against edge with a sickening crack. She snatches the knife from his boot and some part of her mind is shouting to keep him as a hostage, use him as a bargaining chip, but she buries the knife in his throat.

His eyes widen, then go glassy; his body slips down the crate, legs sprawled, arms limp.

Through the scream of adrenaline and ringing in her ears, Gia's focus expands out to the room. She turns slowly, Saint's blood on her hands, to see Tevi watching her with a shocked look on his face.

And behind him, a semicircle of well-armed cartel members. Every weapon is aimed at her head.

Just then, the world explodes.

15

STARLA

O kay, so this is fun.

The forklift operators led the first charge into the passenger terminal — and through a thoroughly surprised pack of cartel soldiers. Starla commandeered one of the pallet-jack-mounted cannons and grabbed Mona's arm; they staked out a spot and started shooting.

While she'd been outfitting the forklift suits with flamethrowers, Absolon had been modifying the cannons to shoot the bungee-type nets dockworkers use to hold down cargo. Starla's first shot goes wide and sends the pallet jack careening back into the wall — she didn't think to set the brake — but Mona reloads it and Starla fires again, the weights on the net flaring wide before colliding with a group of cartel gunmen, tangling them together in a lumpy knot that would be more amusing if the walls around her weren't being scorched black by energy blasts and the air didn't stink with blood.

The passenger terminal is chaos.

Farther down the promenade, dockworkers have blasted open another of the bay doors and are heading off the cartel soldiers who are on the run from the flamethrowers and flinging nets that poured out the door Starla blasted open. Amid the chaos, Starla finally spots Gia and her doctor. Saint is on the ground with blood running from his throat, but the doctor looks badly injured and Gia won't last long fighting off five soldiers. Starla takes aim and snares two of Gia's opponents just as they're about to shoot her, but now she can't use the net cannon anymore without snaring Gia, too. She shoves the controls into Mona's hands and breaks into a run.

Fighting in real life is nothing like in the gym sparring with Gia.

It's at once easier and more incredibly complicated. For one, despite the constant crossfire, nobody is paying specific attention to her. One man turns to fire an electric barb at her as if an afterthought, but before he finishes pressing the button he's hit by a blast of flame from the yelling woman in her modified forklift suit. The barbs flail widely off target. Starla gives the woman a thumbs up. The woman grins and aims her flamethrower elsewhere.

The man who is about to sink his knife into Gia's kidney doesn't see Starla coming, and she stomps as hard as she can on the side of his ankle. It crunches beneath her boot and he drops to his knees, face contorted. She kicks the knife out of his reach, then ducks out of the way as Gia shoves her other assailant off, sending him flying past Starla. Gia yells something that Starla misses, then grabs the man Starla kicked by the back of the neck and slams his head against the wall. He goes down cold. Gia grabs the pistol from his holster and fires it into the third soldier's chest, then aims it at the man Starla disabled.

He lifts his hands and Starla binds them with the disposable cuffs a dockworker tosses her way; Gia slumps down the wall, exhausted, the pistol dangling from her hand.

The room reeks of scorched metal and burnt hair and blood, emergency lights flash red and angry. The surge of union workers has pushed the bulk of the fighting farther down the terminal and into the main station, and almost as suddenly as the fighting started, it's calm. At least where they're standing.

Starla scans the scene. One of her forklift operators is crumpled in his suit, a white-coated nurse bending over him. Three others are sprinting towards the far end of the passenger terminal to help with the fighting there, and she can't see the other two. Presumably they've already spread with the tide of the battle through the corridors leading to the rest of the station as the union sweeps over the cartel.

People are moving slowly through the aftermath of the battle. The medics, helping wounded union and cartel soldiers alike. Dockworkers apprehending prisoners — mostly wads of cartel soldiers tangled up in bungee netting.

It's over.

Starla's mouth is dry and tastes of metal. Her hands are shaking.

It's over.

She spins, looking for Mona, and sees her ducked behind a pile of crates. Good, she didn't rush out to do anything stupid and get herself killed. Starla motions her over.

Gia is at her doctor's side, but she looks calm, not worried. In the last two years Starla has learned to discern how someone is doing based on Gia's expression: this man is going to make it through.

Gia catches her looking and holds out a pair of scissors. "Give me a hand," she says.

Starla looks from Gia to the retreating battle. She'd sent people armed into that fray. She should be there for them. She should be helping.

Gia waving in the corner of her vision pulls her back. "You can't do anything more out there," she says. "This isn't our fight."

Finally Starla drops to her knees beside the doctor and takes Gia's scissors.

"Finish wrapping his leg, nice and tight," Gia says, miming tying the bandage. She turns away from Starla to say something to the doctor, and whatever it is makes him laugh.

"Go, help somebody else," he says — Starla thinks he says — with a smile. "I'll live." Gia leans in suddenly, unexpectedly, and for a second Starla's heart stops: Gia's collapsing, hit by a bullet, maybe.

But, no. She's darting in for a kiss.

Starla looks away quickly, meeting Mona's delighted gaze. They've definitely solved the mystery of where Gia stayed last night.

Gia stands and glares at them both, then points at Mona. "You're with me," she says. "Grab that med bag."

Starla leans over the doctor's leg, wrapping and cutting the bandage, then tucking the end tight, proud of the skill she's acquired over the last couple of years, even if she feels a small pang at having learned it through such awful repetition. She sits back and looks at the man, who's clearly been saying something to her. Oops.

Starla taps her ear. "I'm deaf," she signs.

His lips part in surprise, and he gives her a small nod of understanding. He taps his chest. "My name is — " and he fingerspells it, *T-E-V-I*. It's clear he's pulling the letters screaming from the recesses of his memory, but they're right. Or at least they spell a name.

Starla smiles in encouragement and fingerspells her own name.

"Nice to meet you, Starla," he says.

Across the room, Gia and another of the medics are conferring. Gia looks oddly relaxed — more so than Starla has seen her in years. It strikes Starla that maybe this is her element, consulting with others on the team about more serious injuries, handing out orders and coordinating supplies.

She feels a politely tentative touch on her shoulder and turns back to Tevi. He taps his chest and points across the room.

"Help me walk?" he says, relatively clearly. "I need to help them."

She nods and pulls Tevi to his feet, supports his weight across the room and helps him sit on a stool someone else pulls up for him.

She catches his "thank you" but not the rest as he turns his head to talk to someone else — presumably the rest wasn't meant for her.

She goes to find Mona.

Even with the strike and battle over nearly as soon as it had begun, it's nearly a week before the docks are repaired enough for anyone to leave Maribi Station. That's the official word, anyway. The hole Starla blasted in the bay door was repaired within the first few days, but Starla's heard from Mona that the new bosses are holding things up, not wanting to let a bunch of cartel members or sympathizers escape until they're sure of everyone's identity.

Mona's escape plan hasn't changed, even with the new bosses. "The union's not any different — just a different name," she signs, speaking aloud for Gia's benefit.

Starla glances around, but no one seems to have heard. Then again, it's probably plenty loud here. They're in the Nebula once more, having managed to drag Gia out of the clinic for a drink at long last. Starla has barely seen Gia these last few days; she's spent most of her time at the medical center filling Tevi's role while he heals. He was the only real surgeon on the staff, and the glut of new injuries from all the fighting has kept Gia busy.

She promised she'd relax if she came out with Starla and Mona, but she looks as tense as ever. It's the Nebula's dark corners, maybe, the hologram asteroid tables, the way your brain keeps insisting that you're floating even though you're sitting firmly in gravity — Starla loves it, but Gia doesn't exactly look like she's enjoying herself.

"At least the union will probably treat the people at the bottom better," Starla signs.

Mona's shrug is liquid, her eye roll vivid.

"Maybe. But they still won't let anyone have a real choice around here. Anyway, I'm not sticking around to find out."

"Come with us," Starla signs. "You don't need to stay on New Sarjun, but you can at least ride with us a while."

"I already have a ticket to Toro Station on the *Four Silver*," Mona signs.

"Sell it. Trade it. I'll pay your way with us."

Starla can see Mona thinking about it, see her about to cave, and she knows from experience it's not even a matter of coming up with the right argument — she just needs to ask enough times.

At least, that's what always worked when she was trying to talk Mona into some scheme when they were kids.

"Come on," she signs with a wink. "It'll be fun."

Mona's shoulders rise with breath, lower, and she finally nods. "I hear your planet's ridiculously hot," she signs.

Starla grins. "It's terrible," she signs, but in the joke she realizes just how much she misses it: the way the stars look through atmosphere, the way the sun beats down. Misses them: her family.

"You'll love it," she tells Mona. "We can share a room on the ship. They're cramped, but it'll only be for a few weeks."

Gia shifts forward then, suddenly, fingers steepled and mouth set in a serious line. "You can have my ticket," she says to Mona.

Starla stares at her in surprise. "You're not coming back?"

"No, I am. But." Gia takes a long sip from her cocktail bulb, then sets it awkwardly back on the hologram asteroid table. "I've already talked with Jaantzen about it. It'll only be until Tevi can take over his shifts again. I can't let them work shorthanded with so much going on."

Starla raises an eyebrow with a smile. "Just until he can take over his shifts, hmm?" She lifts her hands in surrender at Gia's glare. "But seriously. You are coming back?"

Gia's nod is slow to come. "To New Sarjun, yes. We'll see what happens after that."

Starla stares at her a moment, slowly letting it sink in. Gia, the fearsome lioness protector of their little crew, is moving on.

It seems . . . right.

Hugging Gia is surprisingly comfortable, her mentor's rock-hard muscles melting around Starla's shoulders after a few hesitant seconds. She smells like sweat and honey and mint, and her vocal chords vibrate as she murmurs something Starla can't see.

Finally, Gia releases her, holding her at arm's length. "Make sure Manu's keeping up his therapy? And that Jaantzen is sleeping?"

"I promise."

"And don't you dare skip your training," Gia says. "If I'm not there, you've got to have their backs, all right?"

Starla nods solemnly, but it didn't need to be said. Nothing is getting past her to her family. Not anymore.

Gia's expression is serious. "You can handle this," she says. "And if you need anything from me, just call."

"Thank you for everything," Starla signs, and Gia smiles and tips back the rest of her drink.

"Of course, kid," she says, getting to her feet. "Now you two get out of here — I have work to do."

EPILOGUE

It's a thirty-second clip, and Gia's watched it a dozen times since she came back from her shower and found the alert blinking on her comm. By now, she's not even bothering to hold back the tears.

The clip starts shaky: blurs of blue and tan furniture and a blinding flash of sun through window before the lighting levels auto-adjust and the camera focuses on Oriol. He's standing in the living room of Manu's apartment, filming himself at a bad angle, his pale face backlit against the window.

He can't keep away the grin as he greets her.

"Hey, G, hope you're doing well. I figured you'd want to see this." His grin widens, eyes sparking gold as he pans away in another blur of furniture and sunlight.

Manu is standing — *standing* — his legs strapped into braces, one of Oriol's crutches under his good arm as he takes his first steps.

And every time she watches this part, Gia forgets to breathe. Manu walks the length of the couch, then looks at the camera and smiles, pain etched into every line of his face.

"You probably thought I'd be slacking off without you here to yell at me," he says. "But I want you to know I've been doing all those goddamn exercises you told me to. Every single day."

"Not every day." Oriol's voice from offscreen.

"You said you wouldn't rat me out, babe," Manu calls back. "He's a liar, Gia. Anyway, I just wanted to say thank you. Come on home safe, okay?"

The clip cuts off again, and again Gia's finger hovers over the icon to replay it, and then she realizes she's not alone. Tevi clears his throat, and she twists on the couch to find him standing in the doorway. She turns away, dashes a hand over her wet cheeks. They're heating with embarrassment at her display of emotion.

"A patient?" Tevi asks, coming to sit beside her. He lowers himself carefully on his good leg and his hand slips comfortably onto her thigh. The sharp, medicinal odor of the clinic still clings to him, but beneath it she catches hints of cedar and honey, and she fights a sudden impulse to bury her face in the crook of that brown neck and let him wrap his arms around her. Let him comfort her like a little girl.

She slides the comm away from her as though it'll erase the fact that he saw what she was watching.

"He's . . . a friend."

The hesitation is because she might have called him a co-worker to anyone else, but using that word here just reminds Tevi who she works for. And lets him paint Manu with the same dark brush he's painted Jaantzen with before the two of them even meet.

The half truth ties itself in a knot and settles in her gut — and trust is a rope only so long, even the tiniest lie knots it just a touch shorter.

"Just a friend?" Tevi asks, misinterpreting her hesitation.

She nods. Maybe she'd had thoughts on him when they first met, but she'd been too bitter and Oriol so sweet, and in the end she knows it wasn't even a contest. And if it had been, Manu made the smarter choice for the long run.

"What happened to him?"

Same bitch that happened to me, Gia thinks. Thala Coeur may have torn Gia's life apart metaphorically, piece by piece, but with Manu she got physical.

"Moto accident," Gia says "What do you want to do tonight?"

They both have the night off, the first time in the weeks she's been here that they're not slipping past each other in their off hours. Yet while they might not have had much time together, those stolen moments have been well spent. And if they're both showing up to their shifts a little sleep deprived and giddy, nobody has commented.

Gia hasn't minded the work itself one bit. She'd forgotten what it can be like at a normal job, where the life-and-death scenarios are limited to the imagination of human cells, the animal malice of viruses, some unfortunate accidental contests between flesh and machine, and the occasional bar fight. She's treating wounds that weren't made maliciously, getting to the root of her patients' maladies by prescribing antibiotics and rest rather than assassinations.

She still finds herself stunned by it on occasion — how wonderfully boring it is.

And the best part of all is that when she stitches up a dockworker's hand or sets the broken arm of a child who fell from the kitchen counter while trying to grab sweets from a high shelf, she won't be seeing them again. She's not fixing them up to send them back out into the fray, so they can return to her with an even worse injury.

Tevi is still on crutches, but just barely, the bullet wound in his thigh healing up nicely. She insisted on being the one to treat it because — Lord knows — she has the experience, but also because she feels responsible. She said that, once, and he responded that he'd known the risks when he brought his team out to the docks. He hadn't quite known the risks of bringing *her* along, though, had he?

Because she was — and still is — Jaantzen's woman on Maribi. She hasn't been asked to do much since the first flutter of messages and meetings, but the expectation is still there — hanging over her head — that she'll help out as needed for as long as she's here.

It's continued to be a sticking point for Tevi, though she tries not to talk about it. A naive part of her wonders if they can just leave this topic be forever. Wonders if there's any universe where building a life together can happen without ever having to talk about the past.

They go back home together, they're gonna have to figure this out.

"Did you get your ticket today?" Tevi asks, like he's reading her mind.

She blinks at the suddenness of the question, then shakes

her head. It was the only task on her list today, besides going to the gym, but somehow she hadn't quite managed to find the time.

"You said you were getting stir-crazy," he says, surprised. "Not that I'm trying to push you out."

"You want your bed back?" Gia teases.

"Not at all. But I might want a bigger one, if you're going to stick around."

Tevi's apartment wasn't meant for two people to share for the long term, and the bed is no exception. It wears off quickly, the ability to share a single bed with another person, no matter how much you want to press your body against theirs. In that way, their opposite shifts have been a blessing, giving them enough time together without spending too many nights trying to actually sleep in the same bed.

"You could," Tevi says. "If you wanted. Stick around, I mean."

Gia's mouth tightens, and he squeezes her thigh.

"I'm only going to be here another few months," he says. He's watching her, and he doesn't seem comforted by what-ever he sees on her face. "If that's what you want," he finishes. "Because that's what I want."

"Let's play it by ear, okay?" She doesn't know what else to tell him, but she takes his hand in hers.

"I was thinking today," he says. "About when I get back. I have enough money saved up that I could live for a few years without a salary. And I, or we," — he gives her a sideways look — "could get the training center started without too much extra cash. I just heard back from the operations director at the Sulila hospital; she said corporate would help with an equipment donation."

Gia gives him a skeptical look. "Just like that?"

"Not just like that," he says. "There's a vetting process I'd have to go through. They'd need to approve my business plan to make sure they're not funding a competitor."

"So it comes with strings attached."

"Everything comes with strings attached."

"It matters if those strings get in the way of what you're trying to do."

He looks down at their hands, interlaced on her thigh.

"Tevi, I thought your whole point was to be a competitor for Sulila. Training doctors who don't come with built-in corporate indentures."

Tevi takes a sharp breath. "I think I can still manage that."

"Even with Sulila's oversight?"

"Do you have a better idea?"

"Private donors."

"And you know a bunch of rich people we could ask?" Tevi asks.

She doesn't speak, and his expression darkens as he remembers the answer. "I'm not taking money from your boss. Imagine what kinds of strings would come attached with that."

"Not the kind you'd think," Gia says. "But it doesn't have to be from him. We can get introductions. There are plenty of people with money in Bulari who would be willing to support a project like this."

"People whose money I wouldn't mind taking?"

"Probably not. Nobody with the kind of money to make a

difference got it clean. Not Jaantzen, not Demosga, not the Yangs, and definitely not Sulila Corp." Gia lets out a sharp, frustrated breath. "Sorry. This isn't what I wanted to talk about tonight." She squeezes his hand. "What do you want to do?"

"I'm sorry, too," Tevi says. His fingers tighten around hers, and he slouches lower on the couch, nuzzling his cheek into her shoulder. "And what do I want to do tonight? I'm doing it."

"You got any good restaurants on this rock?"

She feels him smile, the muscles of his cheek rasping rough stubble against her bare shoulder, the exhale of his laugh warming her collarbone. "Like a date?" he asks. "You never liked those."

"I'm willing to try new things."

"Mmm. There's a place I've been hearing good things about, actually. I've just been waiting for the right reason to splurge."

"Splurge? Does that mean I have to dress up?"

"Don't worry," he says, and he shifts beside her, his lips following his breath to brush her collarbone. The strap of her camisole slips off her shoulder. "Nobody has formalwear on this rock. You can wear whatever you want."

"Even my scrubs?"

"I know you can do better than that, Giaconda." His hand releases hers, and he pushes himself off the couch, kneeling in front of her with a wince.

"Get up, you're going to hurt yourself," she says.

He looks up at her, a mischievous grin tugging at his lips. "That was a pretty half-hearted protest."

"Gotta say I tried."

"Duly noted, Dr. Áte." His palms slide slowly up the outside of her thighs until his thumbs can trace her hipbones above the drawstring house trousers she's wearing. "You're not starving, are you?" he asks.

"Not for dinner," she answers.

———

Everything shifts in an instant as New Sarjun takes hold of Starla.

At first it's a faint tug in the pit of her stomach — *home* — but then the shuttle bucks and the passengers strapped down around her react with eyes pressed closed, hands clenched tight.

A reassuring message crawls across the screen at the front of the shuttle.

The way Starla's stomach drops is at once euphoric and terrifying. With every pitch and roll, a part of her mind says, This is it, this is the end, be stoic, say goodbye with grace.

She remembers the first time she felt this sensation. The only other time she's felt this sensation. When she was strapped into restraints meant not just to keep her safe, but to reassure her Alliance captors that the teenaged daughter of notorious space pirates wasn't going to do them any harm.

And that time, she hadn't been worried about whether or not she was going to die. Back then, strapped to a seat in an Alliance shuttle, she had been buoyed by rage.

What a difference five years has made — and Gia's training reshaping her from a gangly, scrappy teenager to someone who, though she could still use some work, at least isn't going to collapse into a pile of dry bones the instant she hits gravity.

Of course, terminal staff will be waiting with wheelchairs for anyone who needs extra help. Last time, Starla hadn't been given the option to walk out of the shuttle, even if she could have — she'd been half dragged, half carried by a pair of Alliance guards. And she hadn't landed in the fascinating bustle of Geordi Jimenez Space Terminal, either. She'd been dropped behind barbed wire and bars and concrete walls in isolation.

A lot of things are different this time. This time she's coming home to family.

And she's bringing family home.

Mona will feel the gravity, of course, even after the drug regimen she's been on and the physical training she complained about. It wasn't enough to truly prepare her, but at least she won't go into her first few days on New Sarjun as brittle-boned and frail as Starla had felt. Starla's seen to that.

Her stomach drops again with the shuttle, and she fights down her body's panic response. People do this all the time, she tells herself. Ten times a day, and when's the last time you heard about a shuttle going down? She can't think of one.

She rolls her head to see Mona in the chair next to her; her cousin's eyes are wide, her lips bloodless. She swallows, hard.

Starla waves a hand for attention. "Are you going to throw up?" she asks. She signs it with a smile, like she's teasing, but she'd also really like to know the answer before Mona loses it all over the shuttle.

"I'm fine," Mona signs back, but she has a bio bag tucked under her thigh, close to hand.

A safety notice scrolls across the screen at the front of the shuttle, reminding everyone to prepare for the descent, in case they hadn't noticed what was going on.

Mona squeezes Starla's knee to get her attention. Her far hand is digging into her pocket. "I have something I wanted to give you," she signs.

"Now?" Starla asks. "We're not gonna die. People do this all the time."

Mona doesn't respond to that. Instead, she pulls free a delicate chain, the links chattering against each other, spilling out of her hand and dancing a ragged jig in time to the movements of the shuttle. A particularly violent thrust slams both girls into their seats, and Mona's grip tightens on the necklace.

She takes advantage of the following lull to place the necklace in Starla's hand. It's stone, a smooth oval that nestles perfectly into the heart of her palm, and Starla knows — without looking, she knows — what's carved on the other side.

For a moment, Starla's stomach plunges in a way that has nothing to do with the descent.

She turns the pendant over to see the carving: a stylized winged figure coiling upwards, more emblem than artwork.

She feels the cold stone pulling the heat from her body, and for a moment her feeling of being two people at once — now-Starla and then-Starla — is amplified. A girl who thinks she knows what the world has to offer and desperately wants it all, and a woman who now knows enough to be wary, to be prepared. A girl torn free and set adrift, and a woman who's gotten herself a paddle and the will to learn to use it.

All that from a simple stone necklace.

Her mother's necklace.

"Where did you get this?" Starla asks. The shuttle jostles again and the stone leaps from her palm. Starla clutches her fist, fingers snarling in the chain before it can get away. She takes the necklace in both hands, holding it to her chest until the turbulence smooths once more, then she puts the chain over her head, tucking the pendant safely down her collar. She can feel it cold on her sternum and refusing to warm, like it has drunk in five years of grief and locked it deep inside its heart.

"Where did you get this?" she signs again when Mona opens her eyes.

"My mom had it," Mona signs. "I guess the chain had broke? She was going to repair it for your parents, for when they returned to the station, but . . ."

Starla nods; she doesn't want Mona to continue. All her most painful memories are held in that gesture, that trailing off of the fingers. She doesn't need Mona to spell it out for her.

"Thank you," she says, reaching to take Mona's hand. The two girls hold on as long as they can, until the shudders of the shuttle returning to gravity make it impossible and they plummet toward home.

ACKNOWLEDGMENTS

The more I write, the more the community of readers and writers I meet grows — which makes writing this acknowledgements section ever more of a challenge.

An enormous thank you to everyone who has told me they couldn't wait to hear what happens to Starla after reading *Starfall*. Whenever I got stuck on this book, it seemed like someone else would come forward and tell me they wanted to know what happened next. That kept me going through many a rough writing and editing session.

The actual act of writing may be solitary, but I've been blessed with an incredible community of writers in Portland and beyond.

Thank you to everyone who's written with me at the Monday Night Write-In, and to the various brain trusts who have helped me strategize about both business and plots over the past years: my powerful Trifecta ladies, my Tiara Club guys, the Indie Finishers group, the Stone Table's distracting

Slack channel, the Oregon Writer's Network, my #VanSushi lunch friends, the Writer's Social crowd, and my freelance accountability ladies. This would have been a much harder road without you all.

Through writing my Durga System books, I've come to rely heavily on two people. *Deviant Flux* — and all my books — would be way more of a mess if not for their valiant efforts.

First is my husband, Robert Kittilson. Thank you for never letting me get away with a half-baked character motivation or poorly thought through plot idea. I never could have dreamed up a partner as perfect for me as you.

Second is my editor, Kyra Freestar (Bridge Creek Editing). Thank you for continuing to push me and my writing, and I'm sorry it took me so long to start codifying world and character details. Thank you for whipping my mess of a Durga System universe into order. You are a goddess, ma'am.

And, of course, thank you to the incredible Fiona Jayde (fionajaydemedia.com) for the gorgeous cover!

Lastly, thank YOU! I hope you enjoyed this book. If you did, it would mean the world to me if you left a review or told a friend. It's the best way to help an indie author get the word out.

Cheers!

Jessie

ABOUT THE AUTHOR

Jessie Kwak is a freelance writer and novelist living in Portland, Oregon. When she's not working with B2B marketers, you can find her scribbling away on her latest novel, riding her bike to the brewpub, or sewing something fun.

Learn more about me (and get free books!) by signing up for my mailing list at jessiekwak.com.

THE BULARI SAGA

A DURGA SYSTEM SERIES

Book 1: Double Edged

Thala Coeur — Blackheart — is dead. But Willem Jaantzen's relief is short-lived when he realizes she's sent him one last puzzle from beyond the grave. As he and his crew are plunged back into a game he thought they'd left far behind, one thing becomes painfully clear: this secret isn't just worth killing for. It's worth coming back from the dead for.

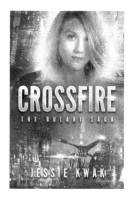

Book 2: Crossfire

The Bulari underground is back at war, and Willem Jaantzen has the sinking feeling the only way to end it is to betray the people he loves the most. And as his goddaughter, Starla, chips away at a seemingly unrelated mystery, bringing peace back to Bulari is quickly becoming the least of his worries.

Keep an eye out for the rest of the series:

jessiekwak.com/durga-system

THE DURGA SYSTEM SERIES

STANDALONE NOVELLAS

Starla Dusai is fifteen, deaf and being held as an enemy combatant by the Indiran Alliance. Willem Jaantzen is a notorious crime lord about to end a fearsome vendetta — and most probably his life. When he learns his goddaughter has been captured by the Alliance, will he be able to save her? And her, him?

Manu Juric's quick wit and knack for creating unexpected explosions has taken him a long way in the hitman business.

At least, until he signs on to a job that might just be out of his league: taking out one of Bulari's most notorious underworld figures, Willem Jaantzen.

Find bonus Durga System stories and more:

www.jessiekwak.com/durga-system

ALSO BY JESSIE KWAK

It's been years since the Ramos sisters have been close, but when Patricia is accidentally possessed by Valeria's dead boyfriend, Marco, they have one last shot at working out their differences. But with a drug smuggling gang hot on their heels, will they have time to heal their relationship?

From Razorgirl Press.

Worried about the state of business during the zombie apocalypse? You're not alone. This humorous collection of zombie short stories proves that festivity and productivity can still coexist alongside weapons trainings during hard times. It includes pieces previously published in _McSweeney's Internet Tendency_, _Bikes in Space 3_ (_Pedal Zombies_), and _Mad Scientist Journal_, along with illustrations by Natalie Metzger.

CPSIA information can be obtained
at www.ICGtesting.com
Printed in the USA
FFHW021940030319
50802255-56217FF